END OF THE EMPIRE

DENISE OHIO

end

of

the

empire

ST. MARTIN'S PRESS
NEW YORK

Design by Jaye Zimet

Library of Congress Cataloging-in-Publication Data

Ohio, Denise.
    End of the Empire / Denise Ohio.
        p.   cm.
    ISBN 0-312-09282-2
    I. Title.
    PS3565.H58E5   1993
    813'.54—dc20   93-21743
                                                                         CIP

First Edition: May 1993

10   9   8   7   6   5   4   3   2   1

3 9510 2001 3799 3

To Catherine, always

. . . a prize one could wreck one's peace for.
I'd call it love if love
didn't take so many years
but lust too is a jewel . . .

—from "Two Songs," by Adrienne Rich

And with what are these on fire?
With the fire of passion, say I, with the fire of
hatred, with the fire of infatuation . . .

—from the Buddhist "Fire Sermon,"
translated by E. A. Burtt

END OF THE EMPIRE

one

•

WHAT DID JEWEL'S mother die of? For two months, Jewel had tried to stop wondering. What was it? Exhaustion? Dreams turned inward that explode, or go sour and eat away at your insides? Outwardly, Jewel accepted the town sentiment that it was drink, but secretly she believed it was the simplest dreams, like getting a job and a car that didn't break down too often, that had done the killing. They bloomed like an orchid of hate inside her mother and strangled her heart. What does a thirty-nine-year-old woman die of? The doctor wrote "Natural Causes" in the little box on the death certificate. It was the only diagnosis he would make for Teresa Alvera Mraz.

Now, Jewel drove her body against another, crying out as if to drive away the thin familiar face she saw floating in front of her closed eyes. She tightened her thighs around the legs braiding with her own. Sweat covered them both, her mouth felt bruised, the bed sheet was a heap at her feet. She and her lover moved, unlocked, shifted, biting and tasting each other in the solid darkness of the room.

Between cries and the creaking of the bed, Jewel could hear the drops of rain hitting the roof. She depended on the rain; always she could count on it to appear in autumn. If only she could rely on it to wash away the picture dancing in front of her. Late one night last summer, her mother had stayed up until Jewel got home from work. She was sitting in the dark kitchen with a cigarette, every cough sounding like blood rusting in her lungs. A car sped by, its headlights pushing away the darkness, and Jewel could see the bones beneath her mother's skin. Cheek and jaw bones were sharp in the momentary brightness, as if the layers had melted and Mama hadn't the strength to replace them till the sun came up. Maybe the effort of wearing a common pretty face was too much for her. It was too difficult to maintain lips and eyebrows and the barest covering of skin.

Maybe the effort to forget that face was beginning to wear Jewel down. The need to know if her mother loved her was wearing her down, too. Maybe, she thought, love is buried like the speck that makes a pearl, and for most people, the pearl itself is enough. But Jewel wondered if there was a way to peel back the shiny layers and get to the center of it. It didn't matter how small or how ugly it was; Jewel just wished to hold the core in her fingers for one brief moment.

Throwing her head and body back, trembling like a leaf in a windblown tree, Jewel reached deep inside herself, deeper, almost falling in the effort to remember and forget. Mama had given up. Given up. The one who had given Jewel life no longer wanted it, had pushed it away with both hands. This life is too much, her mother had whispered before she died.

When Jewel came, she tasted like red wine and honey.

two

•

AL THE LETTER carrier shrugged and stood in the door of the Diamond Cafe to watch Jewel walk by.

"You try to be friendly," he said loudly as he walked across the cafe, "and what do you get for your trouble? A shoulder so cold it could freeze a side of beef. Give me half an egg salad, Marlene."

Marlene tore a ticket from her waitress book, clipped it to the little wheel for Henry and walked over with a fresh pot of coffee. She walked slowly, knowing speed would never get her any more than two quarters beside a dirty plate.

"Did you get yourself some sleep last night, honey?" Al asked, dropping his bulk onto a stool.

"Enough," Marlene answered, sliding a mug of coffee across the counter to him.

Dante hunched over her own plate. The dining room at the boardinghouse didn't open for dinner until five o'clock, so she ended up here before work. Tonight a man and a woman sat in the first booth. He had stringy long hair and wore a wedding ring and a sleeveless Grateful Dead T-shirt, which showed the home-made tattoo on his left forearm. It was a lopsided heart with the name Sheila printed inside, and the dot above the *i* in her name was a brown oval mole. He had moles scattered all over his arms like chocolate chips. The woman was snuffling into a napkin and now her nose was red and sore-looking. Dante wondered for a moment if that was Sheila, or if Sheila was at home, waiting for him to show up.

"But I do love you," he said again.

Love. Dante sipped the coffee and stared at the napkin dispenser in front of her. Most of the people she had ever loved were dead. Maybe they were the only ones she could love—dead people are so much easier to like. She glanced over her shoulder at the couple sitting in the booth. The woman was talking, and Dante could tell by the movement of her head and the tight arch of her shoulders that whatever she was saying was not what the man wanted to hear.

"Jeannie—" he began, but Jeannie cut him off.

Good for you, Dante thought. At least Jeannie knew that if the man was lying to Sheila, he would lie to her as well. For a moment, Dante could see them, two taut ends of the same rope with the middle quietly and quickly unraveling. Suddenly Jeannie gathered up her purse and slid out of the booth, wiping her eyes with the napkin as she ran out of the cafe. Tossing some bills on the counter, the man followed.

"Honey, wait," he called.

Dante heard Marlene sigh. She glanced up at the waitress, then gathered the newspaper scattered on the counter.

"What was that all about?" Al asked. "Joey been messing around on Sheila?"

Dante wondered if Sheila knew where Joey was and who he was with. It was too easy to imagine Sheila standing at the door of a trailer or peeking out the window to see if he had turned the corner for home yet. Dante knew that love could do that to you. It was a firecracker, a barn-burner, a pyre waiting for a woman to leap in. Love made a woman burn bridges she didn't even know about,

4

leaving her with tears in her eyes, a faint feeling of progress and the smell of smoke.

"You done with sports?" Al reached over to grab the paper.

Dante slid it to him, then scooped up a mouthful of coleslaw.

"You got the astrology part there?" Marlene asked him as she topped Dante's cup with coffee. "Why don't you read my horoscope for me?"

Al folded a section of the paper. "I'm telling you, Jewel Mraz could use a little comedown, the way she acts."

"Just because she doesn't say hello doesn't mean she's not a good girl. Now go on and read it."

"She's a snob."

"Jewel's a pretty girl. She's allowed to be a little proud." Marlene set the coffeepot on the burner. "Now read. I'm a Capricorn."

"Thinks she's too good for everybody and she's nothing but a simple slut."

Marlene balanced her hip against the steel counter that ran along the back wall. The look on her face would mean unemployment if the boss was to see her. Lucky she was the boss. "Read the horoscope, Albert."

"After what she did in Tahoe, you'd think she'd be too ashamed to show her face."

Dante looked over the rim of her coffee cup and caught him with her one eye. "What'd she do in Tahoe?"

Al squirmed. It's not right for a woman to wear an eye patch like some kind of pirate or punk rocker. She should get one of those glass eyes like Sammy Davis Junior and quit making people so uncomfortable. "She told everyone she was going to Los Angeles to do some modeling."

"Albert, if you really want to repeat all of that, I could mention a few skeletons I've met in your closet." Marlene's voice was as hard as the stainless steel she was leaning against.

"She asked, Marlene."

"And you just can't wait to tell, can you?"

The door opened, the cool autumn air slipping into the warm diner.

"Hey, Marlene," a man in a sand-colored uniform called as he walked to the back booth.

"Afternoon, Sheriff Tollett. Usual?"

"Make it a bran muffin instead of pie. Got to watch my cholesterol. How's the insomnia? You quit drinking coffee?"

"Yeah. It didn't help, though."

He stopped in the aisle behind Dante, his belt creaking. "Have you ever tried valerian? My wife found some up at the health-food store in the mall at Susanville. Worked like a charm."

"I don't take tranquilizers."

"It's not a tranquilizer. It's a root. It's natural. You should try it."

Dante felt a firm tap on her arm. Don't get uptight, she thought, looking over her shoulder at the sheriff.

"That your bike out there?"

Dante sipped her coffee. Stay calm. "Yeah."

"Nice. Real nice. Used to have a 1932 Indian with a sidecar. Real leather, the whole thing. I sure like American bikes, shame they don't make Indians anymore. How do you compare Harleys with other bikes?"

Dante shrugged, turning around on the stool to face him. "I looked at a crowd of them before I picked that one."

"I test rode a Tour Glide Ultra Classic, your basic Hell's Angel dream bike with all the comforts. Fairing, saddlebags—hell, all you need is a microwave and you'd never have to go home. Very handy and very ugly. Not a beauty like yours out there. Where you headed?"

"I don't know."

"Well, you be careful—the minute somebody gets behind the wheel of a car around here, they quit paying attention to motorcycles."

"I will, thanks." Dante watched him walk back to a booth, then

6

turned to the counter. Nice guy, she thought, getting back to her dinner. Usually when a cop wants to chat it's to suggest a good time for me to leave town.

"How long you been riding those things?" Marlene asked.

"My big brother used to race dirt bikes. He taught me how to ride when I was eight." Dante took a swallow of coffee.

"You'd never get me on one of those things," Al said. "You got no protection if you get in an accident. You're just another road kill, a big old pile of fur and bones in a leather sack."

He barked out a laugh. Dante took another mouthful of coffee, letting it sit for a moment while the hot bitter taste coated her tongue and teeth.

"Good to see you buying American," he continued. "Made in the good old U.S. of A. People buying Japanese cars and motorcycles and television sets to save money don't understand they are saving themselves right into another Great Depression."

The way he said "Depression" with a long, twangy first *e* made Dante want to pour ketchup in his lap.

"Japs make me nervous. They've decided to take over the world by economic domination. They already own half of this country."

Dante fought off the urge to lift her eye patch and aim the scar tissue that had once been her eye in his direction.

Marlene ambled after the sheriff with the pot of coffee and a mug. Al narrowed his eyes as she passed, then he looked back at Dante.

"I was at my Korean Veterans Reunion in Lake Tahoe last spring and I saw that girl dancing in a strip joint."

Dante wiped her mouth with a napkin. "Who?"

"That Jewel Mraz. I saw her in a strip joint."

"Order up," Henry called, tapping the bell. Marlene glanced at the two of them as she set a bran muffin in front of the sheriff, then sauntered back to the kitchen.

"She was the peep-show dancer." His voice was low and urgent. "You know, you go into the little booth and put quarters into a little machine. The window slides up and there's a woman in there dancing at you. I saw her with my own two eyes, wearing nothing but a little corselet and no bottoms. You could see it all."

Marlene appeared in front of Albert, and he leaned back on his stool. She set a plate in front of him. "No need to bring that up," she said, her voice low. "We've all heard it a million times."

"We were just talking," he protested, pointing at Dante. "No crime in that, is there, Bernie?"

The sheriff grunted, not lifting his eyes from his newspaper.

"If a mail truck, a police car and a fire engine come to an unmarked intersection, you know who gets the right of way?" Albert asked, trying to sound jaunty. "The mail truck, ain't that interesting?"

"No," Dante answered.

Marlene shook her head and walked away.

"Jewel Mraz had on no bottoms. Not a stitch," he whispered to Dante as he sprinkled salt all over his food. "She bent over, practically in my face."

Dante studied him. His face was a mix of pastels: pink skin, small yellowish teeth that pushed out too much in the front giving him a rabbity look, square gray-framed bifocals and eyes pale blue, as if he had a drop of milk in each one. His lower lip puckered out in disapproval at the story, but his voice had an undertone of excitement as he told it. Albert shoved half of his egg salad sandwich into his mouth and slurped at his coffee. Dante had met people like Al before. He was the kind of man who, if he found out that his boss was a necrophiliac child molester, would ask to see the pictures. "What were you doing in a strip joint?"

Al's chewing slowed to a stop as he stared at her. He was so fat, she couldn't see his Adam's apple move when he swallowed. "What?"

"I said, what were you doing in a strip joint?"

"Ha!" he laughed, looking around the diner and shrugging his shoulders. "I was at my Korean Veterans Reunion. You know, reuniting."

"Yeah. I heard that," she said pleasantly. "But what were you doing in a strip joint?"

He bit a french fry in half and waved his hand. For a second, she thought of a cartoon conductor beating out the rhythm for an orchestra full of cartoon animals. "So you think it's moral for a woman to be showing her snatch to anyone who'll pay?"

From out of nowhere, Marlene swooped up his plate and dumped the food in the garbage can.

"Hey!"

"I just discovered there's a rat in the kitchen. Can't let you eat contaminated food, now can I?"

Al stood up. "You can't do that! Bernie! She can't do this to me."

Bernie didn't even put his paper down. "She's got the right to throw out anybody who's annoying her."

"But I'm a paying customer—"

"Shut up, Albert," Marlene interrupted, "and get out."

Al crammed the other half of the french fry in his mouth. He tried to give the stool a shove but it was anchored to the floor.

"Fifty cents for the coffee," Marlene said quietly.

Dante watched him toss some change on the counter and stomp out.

"I've seen more intelligent creatures running around a barnyard with their heads cut off." Marlene crossed her arms. "You don't always listen to what people say, do you, honey?"

"Uh-uh."

"Good. Gossip gets quite a distance away from truth and fact."

"But that was the truth."

"Not the whole truth. They say Jewel is bad. I don't know about that. But I do know that when she is good, it's the genuine article."

Marlene rubbed her eyes with one hand. Dante noticed that her nails were bitten down all the way, leaving a ring of ragged skin around the tops of her fingers.

"I imagine that dancing naked for men like Albert Borland is a pretty messy way to make money, but there's no work here. No work with any kind of future, no decent jobs anymore with the lumbering gone. Thank god for the orchards and the vineyards; they keep the small businesses like us going for a while." She sighed.

Dante glanced at the round clock above the coffee maker. The hands were arched like halberds and the lines of the Roman numerals were fractured and thin.

"Me and Henry have been thinking about moving to Portland, maybe to California. You been to California?" Marlene asked.

"Yeah."

"You like it?"

"Too many people, too many cars, too much of everything."

"Well, the only thing we got plenty of is nothing, just like that old song. Nothing and rain, and let me ask you just what good is that?" Marlene let out a laugh. "Are you part Gypsy?"

"What?" Dante blinked.

"Gypsy. I thought you were Mexican like half the town, but your skin's too light. You got any Gypsy blood?"

"I don't think so."

"Indian? Irish? Maybe Czech or something?"

"My mother's family was Italian, from Sicily."

"That's where you got your name?"

"No, my dad called me Dante for a different reason."

"Your dad's Italian, too?"

"I don't think so, but I don't really know."

"So you could be part Gypsy."

"I guess I could be, but I really doubt it."

"Huh." Marlene shrugged. "If you were, you could tell my fortune a little more accurately than that newspaper. Slide it over, would you? I want to read my horoscope."

Dante handed her the paper.

"Funny, isn't it," Marlene continued, unfolding it. "Wanting to know what's ahead as if you could change it."

Dante studied Marlene as she shuffled through the sections. Astrology is irrelevant, she thought. The stars are beautiful—when they fill the bowl of the sky, they could almost push a woman into the ground. What else could you ask from them? Maybe the stars have the right attitude, being completely indifferent to human lives. Then again, maybe I should've been born a Gypsy. Gypsies can do amazing things: read crystal balls, lure hunchbacks, teach goats to dance, understand the night sky. Of course, they might also end up in hell with the horoscope writers, tarot-card readers and telephone psychics with their heads twisted around, chin to shoulder blade, so they can only see what's behind them—the logical result of such twisted sight.

Gypsies or no Gypsies, hell or no hell, people everywhere are pretty much the same, Dante thought, leaving some money on the counter and zipping up her leather jacket. We're always looking for signs. "See you tomorrow, Marlene."

Marlene nodded, absorbed in the newspaper.

three

•

DONNIE JAMES CHAMPLIN had black hair, a job as the projectionist at the Empire Movie Theater and an apartment above the garage of his parents' house. He was there right now, playing solitaire and desperately in need of a red three, a black nine and another ten minutes to finish the hand. Fuck it, he thought, tossing down the cards on the beige carpet, grabbing the half-full coffee mug and getting to his feet.

In the far left corner a four-foot-by-four-foot canvas rested on an easel. Donnie walked over to study the painting in the thin November light. He had installed a skylight last spring, but now believing the sun would ever shine again was an act of faith. Just rain and more rain. The portrait was almost finished; the background was sketched in and he had most of her body on canvas. Only the details of her face were left.

Jewel. How beautiful. Got a hard-on the second she sat down to model. Well, Renoir said he used to paint with his dick, why not me? Stepping back, he squinted. The color of her skin was right, though he hadn't seen much of it when she had posed. Jewel had refused to pose nude. Her modesty had surprised him—he'd heard the stories, as had everyone else in the county. But she had the right and he hadn't insisted. Instead, he had taken his sketchbook and had watched her through the windows of her mobile home. He'd gone three times, once before she finally agreed to pose and twice afterward, enough to get the details he needed: the jutting of her hipbones, the chocolate color of her nipples and the triangular birthmark above her left breast.

Through the window above the kitchen table, he stared across the backyards of his neighbors at Jewel's mobile home. Two months ago, during the end of September when there still had been sun and the smell of apples covered everything, an ambulance pulled into the mobile-home park. People scattered about in little clumps had watched Jewel's mother being driven away. No sirens, since a dead woman is in need of no help. Donnie had watched the whole thing with the pair of binoculars he'd bought last June and kept in the third drawer down to the left of the sink. All summer he took them out at night to watch a figure move back and forth in the frame of the windows. Pen in one hand, binoculars in the other, he sketched Jewel's shifting silhouette in the manner of Duchamp's *Nude Descending a Staircase*.

Watching Jewel had inspired his movie, too. There were scraps of film overflowing a box on the floor of the projection booth: bits of old movies, leader, all sorts of images he had hacked off. The more interesting ones he hung from a pin on the wall and spliced together for fun. One night after everyone had left, he fed his film into the projector. It reminded him of watching Jewel, the random movement of her in the windows. He kept collecting more strips of film and, piece by piece, spliced together almost twenty minutes, which he wound onto an old reel that used to hold preview stock. His film was almost complete; tomorrow night he would show it.

Movies are a kind of magic; watching them makes it hard to believe in the ending of something. Death was a special effect, a dissolve, a bullet that could kill six and go around the corner to kill a seventh. Whoever died could be brought Lazarus-like back to life by a flick of the rewind button. Some kind of miracle. Thirty years of being alive had taught him that there are no miracles. There aren't even any fair chances. There is luck, of which he had none, and there is desire.

Donnie stepped away from the table. Leaning against the refrigerator was the special lighting setup he had ordered from New York City. He straightened one of four chrome tripods; they cost a bundle, ought to take care they don't get broken, he thought. He hadn't had a chance to use the new lights since Jewel was reluctant to sit for him again. Still, as long as she worked at the Empire, he'd see her five days a week, and that was plenty of time to wear down her resistance.

Pouring out the last of the coffee into his mug, he turned off the coffee maker. Time for work. For a moment he had an impulse to pick up a brush and begin painting. Instead, he shrugged into his letter jacket, a leftover from high school days, grabbed his coffee and started down the stairs. It was his daily ritual—drinking coffee, fighting the impulse to stay and paint, his thoughts circling around Jewel as the steps from the apartment creaked beneath his weight. At the last stair, he sighed and hopped over a small puddle. If only Jewel knew about me, Donnie thought. About how I feel. I don't care about Lake Tahoe, I don't care about any of the stories, I know she isn't what people say she is. She's exactly how I see her.

The wet grass sloshed beneath his feet. The ground was so full of water it was as if he were walking on a ship's deck. Hunching further into his jacket, he fingered a stub of pencil in the right pocket. The tip was thick and dull from use, the eraser flat against the metal that held it in place. With his thumbnail, he felt the indentations of the manufacturer's name along the side. He pushed his nail into the soft wood, leaving a crescent.

There's a law of thermodynamics that says everything that's together falls apart. Entropy. He believed that law explained him and Jewel. For those hours she posed, they had been on the way. He thought he felt their souls binding together, understood that

14

here was a kind of salvation. Her perfect beauty and his appreciation of it were not coincidences: The best painting I've ever created isn't an accident, he decided, and it's wrong that I have to sneak to complete it. When will she sit naked for me, so still the light seems to be cascading off her skin like water? When will she look at me with love in her eyes? When will she see that I am the right man for her, that I love her like no one else can and that I always will?

Squeezing the pencil in his fist, he walked faster. Getting to the Empire took just minutes since his parents lived a block off the main street. He didn't have a car, so trying to find work in the mills or lumberjacking was out. Not that Donnie wanted to work cutting trees, losing a finger or an arm in some steel-toothed machine, but it was good money. At least, it was when there were jobs. Sad how no one ever told him or his friends about the true cost of living. Layoffs and bankruptcy happened in big cities. Welfare and unemployment went to people who were too lazy to work. But he'd heard about Tim Johannsen and the food stamps, and noticed that not many of the people he'd gone to school with were still around. Gone to Portland or Los Angeles or Seattle, some even to Alaska to try the fishing.

Donnie James Champlin had gotten a job and married. Kathy'd been a high school champion swimmer. He could remember standing up in the bleachers, the chemicals stinging his eyes and the humidity causing him to sweat half-moons under his arms. Go, baby, go, he would shout, his hands clasped like a megaphone around his mouth. The scent of chlorine on her skin faded after they were married. She hated being pregnant. He could still feel the rush of fear that hit him in the balls and spread up around his heart when he found her unconscious one morning on the kitchen floor. His boy, born more than two months early, lay bluish and still in intensive care, the tubes and instruments seeming too big for such a tiny thing. The baby lay there in that plastic bubble struggling to breathe. Donnie remembered hoping his son had inherited his wife's lungs. Go, baby, go.

After his son died, Donnie struggled to catch his breath. He had thought that at his age things should be falling into place, not falling apart. When he lost his construction job, they moved into the same apartment above his parents' garage where they had made love before they were married. He lost his wife one summer day without warning, when she moved to Coos Bay to be by the water, nearer to her element. The days and nights blurred past as Donnie struggled to keep breathing. To pull air into his lungs. Not think about the coming winter, the smell of her skin, the pull of the ocean, where love goes when it's gone and how quickly things can turn. For a while, he concentrated on hating the blue line of the sea visible from the hills when the sky was clear.

The water in the puddle he stepped into was cold enough to make him grit his teeth. Damn it, he thought, wiggling his toes. He hated having wet socks, though by now he knew he should either wear boots or accept wet feet as a part of life. What good did it do to blame the sky for raining or the city for not keeping the gutters cleared?

He could almost hate water for the power it had over him. Streaming into his shoes. Falling on him from the clouds. Taking Kathy. Misting up to take away the light for his painting—that was worst of all. But what was the use in getting angry? Shake a fist at the sky and all a man gets is strange looks from his neighbors.

Donnie glanced at the quiet houses lining the street. He knew just about everybody in town, had watched his friends marry, have children, then divorce—a new rite of passage no one ever told them about. Even if someone had warned him, Donnie James Champlin would still have been surprised by the speed of things. He did everything he was supposed to do, yet none of the rewards he'd been promised if he worked hard and lived a good life had come to him. He hadn't even gotten used to coming home to somebody when Kathy left, and they'd only had a one-bedroom apartment, no house. No real home.

But that would change. The bitterness of the other divorced men at the Old Mill Tavern and a couple of months spent drinking his unemployment checks with his best friend shook him, but he managed to keep breathing. Last summer he'd realized he had survived for a reason. Jewel. He would endure anything for her, he thought, loosening his shoulders till he no longer hunched against the damp. Wonder if she's at work yet? He turned left at the main street, heading for the bright marquee, thinking there was a small, bright flame burning between Jewel and him just waiting to blaze. She can feel it, he thought. He was sure she could. There were signs to prove it. Posing for the painting. The soft summer nights when she would let him walk with her to make the bank deposit. All the rain in the world couldn't put it out.

Stepping sideways against the drugstore window, he skirted a pool of water that stretched nearly across the walk. The puddles tended to get huge because the sidewalks were cracked and twisted, big square plates of cement shifting out of place. No money to fix them. Wouldn't be for years, till the mill started up again or some miracle turned the place into a tourist trap. Twenty years ago an old Hollywood cowboy star had begun to build Enchanted Rodeo—a stupid name for an amusement park, Donnie thought. The county had gotten as far as laying tar for Enchanted Parkway when the cowboy croaked off in his swimming pool under mysterious circumstances. People said it was a Mafia killing, that Enchanted Rodeo was nothing but a front to launder their ill-gotten gains. Other people said the county should sue the cowboy's estate to recoup the cost of the road, but nothing came of it. Now Enchanted Parkway was a weedy two-lane going nowhere, the street signs pointing it out pitted by .22s and BB guns.

The neon letters of the Empire glowed against the dark sky. Show time. Donnie craned his neck to see "GOD" painted at the top of the obelisk. It faded into the red light from the neon, but you could see it if you knew where to look. No one knew how it originally got there, but twice a year Virgil Penhaligan, a paint brush in his teeth and one end of a thin white rope tied around his

17

waist and the other to the handle of a paint can, would climb a rickety metal ladder leaning against the obelisk to touch it up. This ritual led anyone interested to believe that Virgil had painted the word there in the first place. Virgil liked to do that kind of stuff. Years ago, he had painted the ceiling of the theater white to blot out a mural of Icarus falling from the sky. He must've decided it was Lucifer getting kicked out of heaven, Donnie thought, about to plop off the ceiling to punch holes in the seats with his horns and fill the air with the stench of sulfur.

As if the smell could be any worse, he decided. Unlocking the door, Donnie stepped inside the theater lobby and into the damp, choking odor of the building. Sixty-year-old popcorn, grease, wet weather, dust, rotting fabric, all the smells of artificial things dying. He had thought about working the apple harvest this autumn just to get away from it, but had gotten involved in Jewel's portrait. Just bear the stink and the boredom now, he thought as he walked upstairs to the projection booth. The painting is worth it.

four

•

IT ALL BEGAN with *Bonnie and Clyde,* when Clyde drinks a soda with a matchstick hanging out the corner of his mouth. "We rob banks," Bonnie crows later, and the very rhythm of it sank into Virgil Penhaligan's bones and resonated there. Incomplete Bonnie, dangerous Clyde. But it was not they, their friend C.W., or their enemy the Texas Ranger, with whom Virgil Penhaligan had identified himself. After he saw the film for the ninth time in a row, he realized that he was like poor, blind Blanche Barrow, cornered in the hospital room, confessing to the empty air.

That last time, something seemed to break inside him. Virgil realized that he felt compassion for Clyde and Bonnie, even almost admired their stylish violence. That was wrong. Wrong. He had never before let the iron grip of Righteousness become weak enough to accept Evil, not the Evil in movies and not the Evil in himself. Mr. Mendez and Donnie Champlin found Virgil later that night, alone in the back of the theater, sobbing against the wall while his fingers bled from a jagged piece of glass he had used to cut his chest. Rocking back and forth, he stabbed his pale skin and wailed like an animal.

But there was more than the damage done to his skin and muscles. A tangle of images slid into place between his eyes and his brain. For Virgil, time had always stopped at the movies, but now he could feel a sense of inevitable ending. He knew time was running out. The end, like that final scene, a rag-doll dance of death as Clyde and Bonnie are killed in slow motion, was upon him. He, Virgil Penhaligan, would be left like Blanche Barrow, unable to see the Evil in front of his eyes unless he moved quickly.

Since then new movies were banned at the Empire. Such was the power of the Penhaligans. Virgil's sister, Margaret, knew her brother was sensitive to the modern world, had enough trouble adjusting to the speed at which people live. She gave the orders, Mendez made a few phone calls. At first no one went to the theater, but Virgil didn't care. After a bit, Mr. Mendez arranged special showings of good old flicks—*The Blue Dahlia, The Big Sleep, To Have and Have Not*—and people from as far away as Bend would come. But Virgil still didn't care. He waited, he cleaned up after them, he prayed, he watched. The time was soon. The time was coming. There were Signs everywhere. He understood them and he could control them. Hadn't he painted over the falling angel on the ceiling, covering it with six coats till it was almost invisible except for the outline of the hands like elegant smudge marks?

He had known today was going to be a Special Day. What if, he had wondered as he walked toward the Empire, what if we all have a thousand different souls, each with its own heart and will? Finding the One attached to the Lord would be so difficult for the unen-lightened ones, harder than finding a Prophet in Sodom. No, ordinary people do not have a thousand different souls. Only One for each of them. However, perhaps some of us, the Especially Blessed, have Three in the manner of the Pattern, the Triune Godhead; the essences of the Lord as mixed and useful as 3-In-One oil.

He'd found it, a Sign, halfway to the Empire. How strange, he'd thought. Someone had scattered a deck of diamond-backed poker cards all over the sidewalk. The wind tossed them about on the cement, like an amateur player finally folding the last hand in disgust. Virgil noticed the six of clubs first, lying faceup near the pole of the Stop sign, at a slight angle because of the grass. Then the two of spades and a three of hearts. He didn't begin to feel any apprehension till he walked between the jack of clubs and the jack of diamonds across from each other in almost identical spots on opposite sides of the walk. They were positioned so carefully, edges parallel, both pairs of eyes looking up intently, he was sure it was no accident, no chance positioning. The ominous feeling grew when he realized that, as he turned back to glance again at the jacks, he had stepped on the queen of hearts.

Picking up the playing card, he had carefully wiped off the print of his boot and slipped it into the breast pocket of his flannel shirt—a lumberjack shirt, Margaret always called them. It was a Sign, like reading the shape of a flock of birds as they flew south. A Portent.

Now, as he slowly wound up the cord of the vacuum cleaner, he patted that pocket while staring at the floor. There were diamond patterns in the carpet of the movie theater, and strange designs on the walls around the light fixtures that almost looked like spades all stretched out. Perhaps that was what the cards were about. Something about the theater; something about the Empire. For almost a week now he'd had odd twitching feelings about the place. Somehow, the movie theater had changed, had become almost Diabolical. The cherubs in every ceiling corner were beginning to look devious. He couldn't quite understand the sensations he felt, the unease that grew at night when he was here alone. Maybe the Demons of the place have returned to life, he thought. Maybe the Evil done by the people who come here has gathered enough to be a Force.

Virgil knew about the Evil. He had seen it. It was as if the minute the lights went down and the film came up, decency sank like the *Titanic,* seeping into the worn carpet and broken seats he kept trying to repair, down beyond the floor and into the ground itself, letting Evil float on top for all to see. He knew he was receiving Signs of God's Displeasure. Pretty soon God's going to do something Big, he thought. Maybe an earthquake, and all the people not nailed down to the Holy Laws are going to slide right off the edge of the land and into the ocean. They'll all drown like the people who laughed at Noah. That's what this country is—an Ark. An Ark to save the Righteous. A big Ark made of land. God's going to destroy the Disbelievers and bring a Paradise to the rest.

The Bible isn't just literal. I know that. All those snotty intellectuals laugh at Believers. They don't see that some of Us recognize the Symbols and Signs, too. A plague of locusts could be the pollution that hangs in the valleys, killing the trees and turning the sky hazy. Some of Us see it. Some of Us can even see Signs that they can't. They say playing cards are the Devil's picture book, but finding the cards was a Sign. God often hides messages in what others think Evil.

Virgil would stay late tonight, alone, to pray for Guidance and cleanse the Empire. He was sure now as he stood with the vacuum cleaner. The face cards had symbolized the human Evil collected here, and he would have to get rid of it. Perhaps I should spread salt, he considered. Salt is cleansing, why else would Lot's wife be turned to a pillar of it? Smiling softly, he nodded his head. God was right to have confidence in him. Virgil was a true Prophet.

"Thank you, Lord of Lords, my God of all—" he began, interrupted by tapping on the front door. Jewel. The thought of her made his face burn, caused his tongue to stumble over his teeth. Sinner who would turn to him for Grace and Forgiveness, she stood at the door with her hands in her pockets. Another Mary Magdalene who would seek him out when she turned to Righteousness.

Jewel tapped at the door again, thoughts boiling in her mind. That stupid Albert Borland has his tongue practically hanging out so far you'd think he'd have shinier shoes. I wonder if men like him

22

know how disgusting they are, she thought, catching her reflection in the tall glass doors. They're loud. They smell. They have hair on their backs. And they have the audacity to lean against lampposts asking any woman walking by to suck their dicks. She had heard the proposition so many times in her young life that even if the words didn't come out of a man's mouth, she would hear them all the same.

When she was younger, she'd considered their comments flattering. Later, she still thought of them as compliments: twisted, but sincere. Perhaps men said crude things to her because of the way she looked. She had thick black tousled hair and a beautiful mouth with slightly pouting lips, which looked like she'd given three deep kisses to someone just around the corner. Her height and her sure way of moving kept them at a distance, but her brown eyes gave them hope that if they caught her at the right time, maybe she'd consider a number of interesting positions they could tell their friends about later. Two years before she had left for Tahoe, she'd decided that men who said these things had a mindless, predictable and flabby form of self-restraint, an extremely unattractive quality.

It was going to rain again soon; Jewel could feel the dampness in the air. Besides, it rained more often than not in November. Glancing up beyond the theater marquee, she saw the sky reflecting the rain-soaked streets, two parallel lines of lead and ash without a chance of escape. In the glare of passing headlights, people's faces seemed ghostly and unattached, and time stumbled between splashes of mud and a splatter of rotting leaves. It's hard to think of summer or even of the sun on a night like this, she decided. Everything drags me back to the cold, wet earth.

"Hello, Virgil," she called as he unlocked the door for her. "How are you doing today?"

Virgil nodded in response, not looking at her.

"Might as well leave it unlocked in case I have to go out. I still haven't found my keys. You haven't seen my bag, have you?"

"Yeah." Virgil locked the door, still not looking at her.

"You found it? That's great. Where?"

"In the third row from the front, on the left."

"That's terrific. I can't believe anyone would steal my stuff. What do I have that anybody would want?"

Virgil lifted the black bag from a shelf under the concession stand. Jewel opened it, shuffling through the contents.

"Everything's here. My wallet, my money, my keys. That's weird." She shrugged and closed the bag. Virgil isn't like most men, she thought suddenly as he stood across from her. Maybe there's hope for them, after all. "Well, at least I got it back. Thanks a lot for finding it, Virgil."

He nodded, still avoiding her gaze. "Jewel?"

"Yeah, hon?"

"I'm sorry about your mother."

Slowly, Jewel pulled off her jacket. She shook it gently, then folded it. Don't think about it, she warned herself. In a flash she could hear her mother speaking—you look like your father, you remind me of your father, that sonofabitch—in a deep, dark, gray voice that got weaker and weaker before she died.

"I'd've said something sooner—" he mumbled, then stopped.

Don't think about Mama anymore, she commanded. Not now and not here. "I know, Virgil. Thanks."

Jewel watched him shuffle away. Took him two months, but at least he surfaced into the present long enough to notice. Jewel knew she should appreciate his effort, but she was tired of feeling obligated to people for their false kindness. But Virgil rarely spoke to her; he hardly ever spoke to anyone. He never even seems to look at anybody, Jewel thought. He's like a cat in a world full of dogs, never standing face to face with another human being. Shaking her head quickly, she placed her folded jacket on the shelf below the counter. I'll appreciate his effort later, she thought, gathering up her bag.

Stepping from behind the concession counter, she crossed the lobby. *I have to make sure that hickey doesn't show.* Not that she cared about having one, or the circumstances under which she got it, but at twenty-three, she thought a woman should be over acne and sucker bites. She walked around the staircase, passed Virgil's utility room full of cleaning supplies and toilet paper and opened the door of the women's restroom.

The room was narrow and very clean, though the dim light and cracked tiles gave a different impression. Most of the Empire was red and gold, but not the women's bathroom. An ancient radiator breathed rusted hot air over the once-white tiled walls with their two black stripes running parallel with the floor, one six inches above the ground, the other as high as Jewel's shoulder. To the left, past the three toilet stalls with doors painted a dismal black, was a deep oval sink with worn chrome fixtures. Above it, two lights on either side of a large mirror lit Jewel's face as she studied her reflection. *The buttoned-up collar hides the bite mark pretty well, and the bolo tie is a nice touch,* she thought, smiling at herself.

The room was too hot, the vent always blowing and giving the air the smell of lint, or of an iron that had been sitting too long on the ironing board. The sweet scents of Virgil's floor cleaner and the bar of soap on the soap dish seemed to float on top of the hot air. *Virgil will replace the soap soon,* Jewel thought idly. It was another of his habits, to replace the soap every five days, whether it was needed or not.

Dropping her bag on the counter near the sink, she dug through it for her comb. Not there. *So there is something missing,* Jewel realized, taking out the matching ivory brush. She'd missed the brush. Every night before going to bed, she would light a candle on either side of her bedroom mirror and brush her hair a hundred times. The brushing helped her relax, while the candlelight burned away loneliness. She ran her thumb over the brown bristles then pulled the brush through her hair. She had bought it and the comb out of the Spiegel catalogue when she was still in high school.

Mama had been jealous, she knew. Kept taking them off my vanity or out of my bag. Bet that's where the comb is. Mama thieved it and I'll never see it again now that she's dead.

Dead. The word wiped any lingering traces of a smile off her face. God, oh god, oh god, help me get used to it. The idea of her not here. The memory of looking down at her face that morning. Mama had always been loud; even perfectly still she hummed with energy, crackled with it. Two months, two months and it's not gotten easier to think of her. Mama suffered and sank into death. Maybe she was dead long before she died. Maybe. That night in summer with the headlights passing through the kitchen, maybe that night her spirit left, crossed over, whatever you want to call it. Maybe she gave up the ghost then. But if she was gone before she died, what was that emotion, that desire to protect as I bathed her and sat up with her and fed her and waited for that last breath?

Jewel concentrated on the image in the mirror. She studied her hair. It was almost curly rather than wavy in this weather, and the mist softened it. Her mother's hair had been blue-black, like a movie star's, and she'd only just started seeing the gray when her mother was too sick to keep dyeing it. How embarrassed Mama would have been, she thought, the brush raking through her hair. She hadn't cared if people saw her going to the liquor store, but she would flip out if they saw her without makeup or noticed a single gray hair. Every time she got dressed up, she looked like the captain of a beauty shop bowling team. Jewel smiled to herself. Mama always was one to dress bright enough to stop traffic, and why not? She was still a young woman.

Maybe all those colors had been her protection. Maybe they gave her bravery that lasted more than a few days at a time. Maybe those clothes were a signature of her courage, or a bluff in a high-stakes poker game. Then again, maybe she just liked bright colors.

Jewel pushed her bangs back with her fingers and let them fall.

The humidity made her feel limp. The air from the heat vent made her want to stretch like a cat in the sun. She ran her hand through her hair again, letting it fall in cascading black curves. Her bangs curled toward her face.

Last night someone else had been running hands through her hair. Last night, Jewel's mouth had been kissing and biting appreciative skin. Jewel closed her eyes. Last night, her breasts had fallen forward, letting her nipples, the color of oak leaves in autumn, fill someone's mouth. The sensation glittered in her body, almost sparking along her arms and belly.

She opened her eyes. Some memories become full-length hallucinations, called up by every nerve, every cell, every contortion of muscle. The desire that floated on the surface of her skin made her feel so delicate that the light itself made her shiver.

Virgil stood very still, afraid to kick over the mop bucket or knock a bottle off a shelf and give himself away. The cinder-block wall was chilly and rough under his hands as he leaned against it. His thumbs almost touched, like those of a movie director framing a shot, under the uneven hole that looked into the ladies' room. He loved to watch Jewel brush her hair. Long wavy black strands that circled her face, soft curls she would run her fingers through slowly. He had watched her do it before at home. Hiding in the unkempt shrubbery around her yard, maneuvering carefully through the sharp branches, he could look through the window into her bedroom. She had sat in front of a mirror in a T-shirt, brushing her hair by candlelight, while he watched as if offering up the sight to God with his eyes. He refused to imagine touching it, letting it mix with his fingers, the softness of it wearing down his strength. At first he had thought his desire to see her had been Sinful, Bad, an Evil. But he knew now that God had made her beautiful as a Sign of His Goodness. He knew he was meant to watch this young woman and no other; God had placed her ivory comb in his path. Virgil had found it the night she forgot her bag at the theater. He had wanted to take the brush, but it was too big to carry with him. The comb was the perfect size; he had it now in the bib of his overalls, right over his heart.

Soon, he thought, peering through the small hole in the wall of the closet. Soon, you will come to me.

Donnie James took a sip of coffee, set his mug on the counter and peered again at the film on the splicing editor. He'd already cleaned and oiled both of the big Century 100 projectors, taking special care with the one on the right near the door, since it accumulated more oil and emulsion on the track and tension shoes. All the crud could cause problems with the electronic change-over from one projector to another, meaning an embarassing gap between reels.

He squinted at the sprocket holes on the second reel of *D.O.A.* They were starting to tear again. The splicing tape would probably hold up tonight, but he didn't like the looks of it. Hell with it, he thought, winding up the film with the hand crank. If Mendez isn't going to take care of the old movies, why should I? Too many times, Donnie had come in to find the film was almost useless— poor splices made it jump, or mismatched sprocket holes made the projector start a terrible racket and sometimes jam, causing the film to melt. He used to care about it, but lately the old Hollywood movies didn't seem to be worth a pile of crap anymore.

He screwed the cap back on the carbon tetrachloride he'd been using to clean the film. Donnie loved the smell of it. Some people thought it was horrible. The sharp chemical odor spilling out of the bottle gave Sue Potts a headache. Turk would always stand in the corner with a half-full bottle, sniffing it, though Donnie was sure that was for show. He'd known George Turkmanitz since junior high. They had lockers right next to each other in gym class. They'd been skinny twelve-year-olds ducking out of the way of the bigger guys till they became the bigger guys. Turk had introduced Donnie to acid, Black Sabbath and Kathy.

Donnie lifted the twenty-five-pound film reel onto the projecting arm of the left Century 100. He'd already cleaned the mirrors, Cinemascope lens and lamp house, remembering to slide the brass aperture key back into place. Setting the crank, being sure to leave a finger of film as slack before the sound drum, he threaded the film through the projector to the empty reel at the bottom. Stepping to the power box, he threw the switches to pre-light the lamps and start the vents. The projectors huffed into life while he fiddled with the main volume control. There were four stacks of speakers behind the screen that could throw sound all over the theater; Donnie considered that many speakers overkill. As if anyone is interested in my opinion, he thought, spinning an empty preview reel onto the counter and knocking over his coffee mug.

Lukewarm coffee splashed onto the floor. Shit, he thought, watching the brown stain spread. That was really dumb, goddamn it. I really wanted that coffee. Now it was down two flights of stairs for some pop to get the dose of caffeine he'd need for the night.

Nobody was in the lobby. Stepping behind the concession counter, Donnie poured pop into a paper cup. Jewel's jacket was on the shelf, but she was nowhere in sight; neither was Dante. Huh. Maybe we can go out for a drink after work tonight, he thought, sipping the sweet drink, the bubbles popping against the roof of his mouth. Maybe Jewel and me can slip off later. Be real handy if Dante and Turk get it together. She'd be good for him. Dante was unusual enough for Turk to find her interesting. She was funny and sexy in a leather-and-eye-patch way. Yeah, she was okay. Maybe he himself would've fallen for her if Jewel hadn't been around. Maybe, he thought with almost a regret, if Jewel was still in Tahoe, me and Dante would have had a chance.

Hell, I'm going out with Sue Potts tonight. Could call and cancel. No. Did that last night. He shrugged and walked around the staircase to the closet to get a mop, even though Virgil had a rule that no one could clean up anything but him. Even a drop of water and he was there, scrubbing the spot with ammonia and miracle cleaners. Virgil even wiped all four projection booth windows every night. Somebody ought to tell the guy that the Empire could barely stand all the polishing; the place was held together by dust, rust and general decay.

Donnie shook his head. Virgil Penhaligan is the biggest waste of food I've ever met. First, he's a nut case, thinking because he'd been standing at a certain place during a thunderstorm, he's some kind of Moses from the Bible. But to make it worse, the fucker owns the Empire. Lock, stock and barrel. One of the Penhaligans, with all the Penhaligan money sitting in a bank somewhere. It's more than unfair. It more than sucks. It's a great cosmic joke that Virgil's a rich man and doesn't know how a rich man should act. He's a janitor in a movie theater. A janitor. King of the brooms. Wears greasy overalls and a belt with keys and tools and other junk hanging from it. Has a shaggy Prince Valiant haircut and that pitiful, ragged beard covering half his face. Doesn't own a car. Doesn't even own a bicycle. Walks to work every day, carries his lunch in a paper bag, always says yes sir, no sir, to that creep Mendez.

What does Mendez know about movies anyway? He doesn't know shit. He won't book art films or anything made after 1954. No Eastwood. No Schwarzenegger. No Jason, no Freddie. Jesus, no wonder there are no audiences. A goddamn lawyer playing errand boy for the Penhaligans. Gets the deposit receipts from Jewel, has me unload the movies from the trunk of his car and blam, off he goes. Doesn't offer to help carry the five or six film reels to the projection booth, though the damn things are three feet across and I end up making three trips. Doesn't help Jewel with the boxes of candy, either. Once he even stood there watching her drag a fifty-pound sack of popcorn across the lobby. Guess as long as he can give the Bedbug a job sweeping garbage out of the aisles, he doesn't have to worry about keeping his job.

If the Penhaligan money were mine, there'd be no question what I'd be doing. Own a big house with a studio full of light. Make films, build a recording studio. Travel. Keep an apartment in

New York for when I had to show up at galleries to sell paintings. With Jewel. She'd leap at the chance to be with me if I had big bucks. And I could paint. Paint. Paint and make love. How fine it would be.

Donnie opened the door of the closet and turned on the light. There, hands against the bare cement wall, stood Virgil Penhaligan.

"Virgil? What are you doing, man?"

Virgil rushed out of the closet. He smacked into Donnie, which made the pop spill over the sides of the cup and onto the carpet, and rebound back into the closet.

"Shit! Virgil! Be careful!" Donnie shook his head and flicked the pop off his fingers. "I spilled my coffee in the projection booth. Can you clean it up?"

Virgil grabbed a mop and bucket and scurried away, leaving Donnie alone. Walking into the closet, he grabbed a rag off a shelf to wipe his hand. What was Virgil doing in here in the dark? Praying? Meditating? Jacking off? Though god knows the Penhaligans could hire people to jack off for them if they wanted. Donnie tossed the rag back and glanced at the wall where Virgil had been standing. Unpainted cinder block, the very color of depression. He looked closer.

When Donnie took another half step, he could see the small hole in the wall. He switched off the light, then pressed his eye to the hole. I'll be damned, he thought, amazed. Virgil's drilled a hole so he could look into the bathroom. Jewel's checking out her hair and I can see her perfectly.

Donnie squinted, trying to get a better view. There wasn't much to see at this angle. The hole was on the far right of the mirror, same side as the toilet stalls. Wouldn't really see anything but girls brushing their hair and putting on makeup, but it was still pretty handy. Well, hell. So the righteous Virgil Penhaligan has got a thing for gaping at the girls. Donnie turned away from the hole, a grin on his face. My man is a voyeur. A Peeping Tom. A pervert. He shut the closet door. Who'd've thought it?

Donnie gave Jewel a brilliant smile as he turned the corner to run up the stairs two at a time. Oh, please, she thought. Don't start hitting on me again. Amazing how women can turn men down and they just keep coming back for more.

Reaching under the counter, Jewel took the register key from its hiding place in the box of emergency candles. She'd bought the candles herself after her first week, when she realized that Virgil had hidden every flashlight in the place. Unlocking the till and the sliding glass door of the candy counter, she returned the key to its hiding place and began restacking candy boxes. Milk Duds. Raisinets. Red licorice, chocolate almonds, nonpareils. The new boxes she moved to the front, rotating the older ones back. Need Skittles, Jujyfruits and M&Ms. She double-checked the expiration dates on the Goobers. Oh, god, another batch gone to waste, she thought, pulling the white-and-brown boxes off the shelf and stacking them next to her. Where does Mendez get this stuff?

Jewel bit her lip. Dammit. Why won't Mendez get us some decent stuff and why won't Donnie leave me alone? What is it with him? It's not that I don't find some straight men attractive. I do. But the majority are so damn weak—takes all they have to deal with their own tiny problems. It's as if the very minute they hit puberty, they let their spines melt and drip into their pelvises. Every time they come, they lose a little more backbone.

five

•

DANTE STEPPED INTO the November day. It was dark already. She glanced around the deserted main street of town. Quiet. The streetlights were making a brave effort against the night enveloping the valley, and the clouds reflected an eerie silver-gray as they moved. In certain parts where the clouds escaped one another, fragments of the sky broke through like small, blue crystals of clear intelligence.

Lighting a cigarette, Dante tossed the match into the gutter. Miraculously, it spluttered for a moment before going out.

Dante liked fires. She knew they were destructive, knew people died, families were destroyed and animals got trapped by them, but she loved fire—the heat, colors, sounds of wood giving in and glass shattering. There is ending in fire. Whatever has been done is finished. Emotions explode like glass, events crumble like walls and are devoured. They don't ever return. There is no instant replay. There is no examination. There is only starting over. Erasure and replacement. Fire is controlled violence, passion gotten out of hand and out of bed; it is heat and light and an end.

She had seen a house burn down outside Durango, Wyoming,

33

one night in June. She watched the flames dance and lick against the night sky, wanting to light a cigarette and deciding not to out of respect for the family silhouetted in orange standing in a half-moon in front of the house. She folded her hands over the gas tank of her bike to watch the flames eat the wood and lick the glass of the farmhouse. It was tall, thin, two-storied, with long windows and a porch that caved in with a sudden crash, like someone having a heart attack. From where she sat, she could feel the heat as the flames stretched beyond the height and length of the house. Someone's home going up in smoke.

The flames grasped at the night sky searching for a new grip, fell back, leapt again upward, sideways. The heat seemed to bend and twist the stars themselves, and in the darkness between the fire and the sky, tongues of blue were imprinted on her vision.

The family hadn't turned around when she pulled up, they didn't move at all until the Durango Volunteer Firefighters truck wailed toward them. They swung around when firefighters in fluorescent yellow jackets and helmets with the long brims hanging over their backs spewed out. It was a shame they showed up then. Too late to save the house, but not so late they wouldn't try. They crashed around, unfurling hoses, stomping on the grass and flower beds with their big boots, their voices echoing with disappointment that they would have no chance to be heroes, and relief that they could be brave on the edges of danger.

The family shifted out of the way, the woman leading the man by the hand. The small boy followed, glancing away from the fire to notice her on the shoulder of the highway. He grabbed the man's wrist and motioned toward her. The man looked up; she could see the side of his face as he stared at her and the chrome of the motorcycle glinting and shifting with the fire.

A search for meaning yields hundreds or none. Dante knew the man was searching for something as he took in the details of her watching his disaster. She was far enough away that he would never be able to describe her face, but close enough so he noticed there was something out of balance, something not right. A shadow at her eyes where there should be no shadow. Dante could almost feel his gaze, just as she could feel the heat from the fire. She started her bike and pulled onto the road.

The night air beyond the fire's circle of heat was almost a lash against her face. A kind of despair circled around her throat like a pair of hands. Dante wanted to get off the bike and let her feet sink into the soft ground of the forest around her, but this land was owned; there were signs and fences in front of the trees. A forest fire would save these people from themselves, she thought for a moment, gunning the bike in the darkness. Maybe that's what we all need—to be saved from ourselves.

Dante took a drag from her cigarette and walked slowly toward the Empire. She thought she understood fire. She felt she was a *hibakusha,* an explosion-affected person. The word came from the survivors of Nagasaki and Hiroshima, the people who carried radiation in their bodies and scars on their skin, and like them Dante knew of a world beyond order and flattering shadows. The eye she was missing had sight like no other. How clearly the scars and burns showed on people when she looked at them with that eye. We're all *hibakusha,* Dante decided. Only some want to remember the explosion and some want to forget.

Dante had wanted to forget a lot of things. Mostly she wanted to forget that this life is mirage and the flickering of light. A pull of breath. Another. Then nothing. If there was a reason, it wasn't wrapped in the human ability to weave meaning into the universe with two threads and a sense of self-importance. She wandered the country on the black and chrome motorcycle, stopping at small towns that dotted the countryside like forgotten beads on broken strings of highway. The bike drew attention first, the V-shaped engine between her legs growling for every pair of eyes to take a look. Then the eyes took in the square-toed boots, the legs like licorice whips, the leather jacket and the gloves. Then the eye patch. It was too much for even the most liberal citizens. She had a glass eye, like a marble made by a twisted toymaker, wrapped in a pouch at the bottom of the left saddlebag, but she never wore it anymore. On the bike the wind dried out her skin too quickly and the rattling of the glass eye in her skull left her feeling a little more detached from the ground than she already was. The patch worked well. Six months ago she decided to wear one all the time. Of course, in small towns there are whispers, a word that doesn't refer to volume, but to what is being said and how it is phrased. The whispers about her began immediately, sometimes before she swung her leg off the bike.

Some people find comfort in the familiar. Others seek the challenge of finding something new in it. Dante considered herself the test for everyone who saw her. Which type are you? her body would ask as she walked down a sidewalk. Just how far will you go in making me everything that I'm not? How far will you go to turn me into metaphor?

Plato conceived of vision as a ray of light beamed out of a mind to collect images. The eye takes in images, transposes them into electric signals that the brain reconstructs and interprets. Plato's ray is not a beam of light, but a beam of understanding, and individual meaning is imposed on an image. The sheer number of images scooped up by the eye and sorted by the brain is huge, so huge that the heavy hand of such accumulation pushes people toward a cluttered grave.

And sometimes, an eye sees that a gas gauge is almost to Empty and it's time to forget philosophy and get on with the practical. A week ago Dante had pulled into this small Oregon town for lunch and to fill the gas tank of her bike when she saw *To Have and Have Not* spelled out on the theater marquee in square uppercase letters. Shit, she thought, squinting up. Nobody shows the old flicks anymore, especially the only movie theater for fifty miles. She was wrong.

The Empire Movie Theater was one of those old, single-screen houses with fat-cheeked, gilded cherubs in the lobby, and real, if a bit moldy, red velvet curtains that swallowed unwanted light and sound. The main curtain would swish open—pulled by hand since no one had bothered to repair or replace the machine that would open it automatically—for the please-don't-smoke-or-talk film, close slowly, then open again immediately for the feature. No one was sure why Mr. Mendez kept doing that, but he did. Orders from higher up, no doubt.

There were lights along the aisles, the kind with a slitted cover just bright enough to show the way, yet dark enough so people could relax, dark enough to hide all but the worst of the tears in the seats, the worn spots in the carpet and the water stains on the ceiling. The damage showed only when the houselights were on full, which was why Mr. Mendez warned Dante to never, ever, bring the houselights up full.

"Not even in an emergency?"

"Absolutely not."

She shrugged at his back as he left. Her job was easy. She was to collect tickets, lower the lights and open the massive red velvet curtain, now so frayed at the bottom that Mr. Mendez warned her about it catching on the splintered floor. Of course he didn't know, and she didn't bother to tell him, seeing as he was always checking his watch as if his whole life was running late, that she didn't have any intention of lasting longer than a week or two at the most. She needed a break from the road; he needed somebody to help out. Neither said anything about making it permanent.

Dante took a drag from her cigarette and glanced up at the theater's marquee. *D.O.A.* and *Gaslight* were the films they were showing this week. She liked them, even after watching them both Wednesday and Thursday at the 6:00 and 8:45 shows. She had a favorite scene, a moment, really, in *D.O.A.,* when Pamela Britton, playing Paula the secretary to Edmond O'Brien's soon to be dead-on-arrival Frank, kisses him outside the Allison Hotel in Los Angeles. At the beginning of the kiss, her hands meet in the middle of his back. Narrow, strong, sweetly beautiful hands.

Dante wanted to suggest showing *The Inn of the Sixth Happiness,* another Ingrid Bergman film that starred a cancer-infested Robert Donat, or *Quo Vadis?,* a 1925 silent with three directors and a story line only the Italians could love: dissolute Romans, pious Christians and a lot of hungry lions. Dante had never seen it herself, but it was on so many Worst Ever lists, it was bound to be interesting. She had heard that to make the lions ferocious in front of the cameras, they were starved for days at a time. One of the biggest escaped, leapt into a crowd and proceeded to maul an extra. The animal trainers were reluctant to kill the lion, even after the lion had begun eating the extra for lunch. Finally a keeper took out a rifle and shot the starving animal.

But Donnie James had told her that foreign films were out. Mendez had a thing about proving how Anglo he really was, even to go so far as to cheer John Wayne in *The Alamo.* During Halloween week two years ago, Donnie told her, Virgil had insisted on showing *Nosferatu,* even had Mendez hire Mrs. Bustillos to play a portable organ. Some students from a community college sixty miles away had shown up one night. Reverend Duffy watched it twice. That was it. Mrs. Bustillos was let go after three days, though she was paid for the week. The rest of them—Donnie, Virgil and Gina Bustillos, who had worked the concession stand before Jewel—showed up every night and played that creepy old film to no one. That was what Virgil wanted and that was what he got. After all, the Empire was his.

The neon lights of the obelisk were glowing crimson. The small puddles gleamed like ice from the fluorescent light of the marquee, turning the title of the movie backward. It was repeated in the water caught by the broken corner of the sidewalk, the long shallow pool near the curb, and a still, deep puddle near the drain, where leaves had blocked the holes and the water couldn't get through.

Dante stared at the pools, where the letters floated like a code needing to be broken, then she glanced at the tall glass doors. Virgil kept them polished to such a high sheen, she could look at herself. Black jacket, black eye patch, black hair. One almond-shaped blue eye. The smoke curled away from the cigarette she held in her fingers. Looking past her reflection and into the lobby, she saw it was as clean as Virgil could get it. The crystal chandelier hanging like an upside-down wedding cake cast a rich gold over everything. What it didn't illuminate the chrome light fixtures along the walls did, fixtures that looked like bowls cut in half, with each bowl held up by the arms and wings of an angel. These angels, however, were not Botticelli rip-offs but thin, elegant figures. Dante found the clash between the art deco light fixtures and the cherubs in the corners to be oddly soothing. Maybe because they were tossed together in a movie theater. Theaters have a way of suspending the expected. Theaters were a little magical—dreams could come true, miracles did occur, time stopped.

Dante puffed on her cigarette. Strange to find Jewel here. Strange that she recognized me immediately, even though my hair is different and I wear my eye patch all the time. In Tahoe I was much too self-conscious of my face to wear one during the day. Trying so hard not to be noticed that of course people looked, till I realized that you have to give people something to stare at. A single thing for them to concentrate on. A tattoo that covers your whole body, a strange haircut, going topless down the main street. They get so busy looking at that, they don't even notice you. But of course I didn't figure it out till after Tahoe. Till after I left Jewel.

Maybe there is such a thing as destiny, someone somewhere plotting out all the twists and turns of a lifetime like a spider spinning a web, all knots and purpose. Whoever and whatever it was that pushed us together in Tahoe was doing the same thing here now. Yeah, right.

Touching Jewel was a shock of muscles, the hard curve of hip bones and strong, demanding hands and mouth. Whisking her hair across the back of Jewel's thighs, kissing the sweet skin of her wrists, Dante had locked arms and legs with her as they had sweated and gasped and rocked each other into bliss. Only when she was inside Jewel was there any sensation like silk, enveloped in the slippery skin of her cunt, the spiderweb softness of her skin. She moved her fingers, twisting, spinning her hand, watching Jewel's beautiful face as they fucked. She caught a nipple in her teeth and heard a sharp intake of breath.

She ran her finger around the opening of Jewel's womb. She hated that word, hated the passive, speech-defected sound of it. It was wrong, too soft. Dante could feel the same sensation in her own body, that flickering pleasure from experienced hands. Her cunt reminded her of a sea anemone at the mercy of the tides.

Dante flicked the cigarette away, opened the door and stepped inside the Empire.

Jewel shook her head. Some beginnings are not beginnings. They are continuations. So it felt as she rewound the electrician's tape around the power cable to the popcorn machine. Every night the machine would shudder and hum, its lights blinking in electric epilepsy. She told Mr. Mendez, but he wouldn't get a new machine. Virgil wouldn't replace the cable because he didn't like to mess with electricity, and, considering what had happened, she could hardly blame him. Handing her the roll of tape with the price tag still on it, Mr. Mendez tapped the glass counter with his *Wall Street Journal* while he told her to find the break in the cord and repair it. Now checking the repair was the first thing she did every night after stuffing her jacket under the counter and brushing her hair. Kneeling on the greasy floor, she would carefully rewrap the tape like an industrial tourniquet, while trying her hardest not to think about electrocution. It was a ritual. She avoided the worst grease spots and the cracks in the floor. And never again did she hit her head on the edge of the counter after the first time.

"Jewel?" A soft voice came from above.

She looked up. Staring down at her was Dante.

Six

•

DANTE SAT ON her motorcycle at the Rock Ridge Scenic Viewpoint, gazing out over the valley. This was ranchland and farmland. Because of the fog, she couldn't see the patchwork quilt of old-growth forest and clear-cut that covered the hills. The old two-lane highway was obscured long before twisting up the side of a mountain. So were the shallow gullies that separated asphalt from the trees and tree stumps that stuck out of the ground like rotting teeth. The air was still, and the smell of pine mixed with the scent of wood fires, rain and the sea a hundred miles away.

That sea still tossing our losses up onto the beach. That sea that is the land's edge, hinting at lives and times of earlier creations. That sea reached to these hills once, she thought, just as the Sea of Faith splashed through this valley. But both seas retreated, pulled back— so far back, I'm surprised to see any kind of ocean going on at all anymore. Ah, love, let us be true to one another, the poet says, but he never mentions if we are to be true like the sea or the mountains or the movies or fire itself.

Laying her motorcycle gloves on the handlebars, Dante leaned back on the Harley. It was a cold morning, and a chill made its way through the leather she was wearing. The mist made everything appear as bleary as the vision of a nearsighted woman. Thank god at least it's not raining. All the wetness makes human ignorance shoot up to bloom early, as if the native soil is rich in stupidity.

Glancing up, she noticed the fog beginning to break apart under the sunrise. A layer of clouds shifted, showing the maroon and crimson and cool green of new morning washing away the needle points of stars. I wish I could have a star. I wish I could have a cupful of stars. Sharp and burning, the light bright enough to shine through muscle and skin. Imagine filling a cup full of such a treasure and giving it to someone. Is that what she means by love?

Dante crossed her arms, hugging the warmth closer. I can remember telling somebody once that the difference between lust and love is that when you love somebody, you give her the key to your handcuffs. But now, somehow, I have caught in my mind this idea that as a woman gets older, her heart sheds its leaves like a tree. While trees can return to their greenness, a heart can't. The wind begins to tear away at it; twigs, then branches, till there's nothing left but the trunk and broken ends of limbs standing black against a gray sky. The heart in perpetual winter.

It's so hopeless to have such a heart, and it is painful. Truth hurts. No—more like truth frightens to a state of jellylike immobility and all I can do is stand there and quiver. Sweet singing Jesus, is it love or the lover that I'm so afraid of? Jewel. Darling. Last night as you lay beside me, your body curving with mine, a beam from the streetlight stretched over the windowsill to stroke you from shoulder to thigh. As I watched I thought, there is a promise to me written into your body. But there are no promises. In that room, the bed hurls questions and I have no answers.

Dante studied the line of the hills, round, soft-looking. She wished she were on the other side of them, tearing away from the tiny cluster of buildings in the cup of the valley. Why can't I leave? she wondered. Why can't I just go from this place? Is it love? Is it Jewel? Is it some kind of luck or destiny that keeps me here? Is it gravity or a leash? Is it something I didn't even know existed that keeps me turning round and round her?

She rubbed her face, brushing her eye patch with the tips of her fingers, then caressing cheekbones, nose and mouth. The cold ride up to the ridge hadn't swept away the scent of Jewel. The smell of leather couldn't cover it. Holding her hands before her, Dante looked at the creases in her palms and the whorls of her fingerprints. With these hands I touch her. I please her. If I were her daughter, her sister, her mother, I would never touch her like I do. If we shared anything but what we share now I would never see what her face looks like when she comes. If I were anyone but who I am.

Folding her hands, Dante closed her eye. For a moment she felt that she should recite an old childhood prayer, something with rhymes and confident hope. She breathed in deeply, the air rushing through her teeth. Wood smoke painted the back of her throat, and she could taste the imminent rainfall. She hunched deeper into her leather jacket. There is a surplus of water here, she thought, and these people don't understand deserts. Can't understand the great stretches of rock that cover Nevada and the flatlands of East Texas. Can't understand the long dry summers that leave Dakota wheat fields and cornfields covered in dust. Can't understand the overlook at Death Valley called Dante's View.

Should I go back to the desert to wander like Moses or that Jew who told Jesus on his way to Golgotha to go a little faster? The desert is full of spirits, much fuller than any city or this valley. They fill the air like a fine ash from a sacrificial fire. Should I go back to the sea? The quiet there can't be found anywhere else. Should I go back to the mountains? Should I find a different valley? Should I sit perfectly still in the middle of the interstate and wait for a truck to solve my problems? Dante took another deep breath. Death comes soon enough, why go out looking for it?

Jewel. Should I go back to Jewel? Will I always be returning to her? From now on when I think of her, will it always be last night?

Her mouth. Her hair. Her body as we stretched out naked against each other. Some people think that women touching each other is like silk meeting silk. Some believe it to be all smiles and generosity. They ignore the shape-changing muscle beneath a woman's skin that promises heat and sweat and great strength. We're evenly matched, Jewel and I. Both strong. Both stubborn. Desire hits one and echoes to the other. Delicious, Dante thought, her cunt opening with an ache. Jewel took me by surprise when she slid inside me and all I wanted was to pull her in deeper.

We meet at each other's bodies and that's all it's supposed to be. But last night, when I walked her home and we stopped to kiss in front of the Empire, the huge glass doors brought me a revelation. I looked at Jewel's face and, over her shoulder, I saw her body reflected in the glass. In the periphery, there was another reflection of her. And I think now that while Jewel is not two-faced like most people, she might be two-bodied, like one of those creatures on the corner of a building. A body on the left and a body on the right, sharing a single face like the *T'ao T'ieh,* the symbol for gluttony the Chinese paint on the bottom of their dishes to warn against over-indulgence.

Dante opened her eye, feeling dizzy. Why am I sitting here, letting each stray thought float up like a frail fire balloon in search of a local saint to intercede on my behalf? Maybe I should return to the sea and set a votive lantern afloat on the evening tide. I could stand on the beach, watching the light grow fainter over the dark surface of the water, and hope my gift of fire travels beyond the horizon.

She shook her head and looked around. She knew that to the north were the grasslands dotted with cattle and sheep. South were farms, squares of brown from crops plowed under and strings of pumpkin and squash vines. The vineyards were gray twigs and the trees in the orchards stood like soldiers. Marlene had said that on the last of the warm autumn days, if the wind was blowing right, the sticky sweet smell of cider braided itself into the air.

You can't see any of this from the Empire, Dante realized. Not even on a clear day. All you can see from there is the end of things. Just a line of hills, speckled with rusted bits of machinery seeping diesel and rust, and the switchbacks left by the lumber companies. Already they were being swallowed by the hillsides and the moss. But Dante had the feeling that the neon of the Empire could be seen for miles up in the mountains, glowing like a torch.

Love. Fear. Flight. Desire. These emotions seem to swirl around inside me, sneaking out now and then as bait for some memory. What would it be like to weave a blanket of emotions or piece them into a quilt? To let someone run her hands over the fabric, let it slip through her fingers and drag over her arms. To wrap Jewel in such a quilt of my making. To let her sleep under it. What sort of dreams would she have, and would I be in them? Would I be alone or with her? Would we be wrapped around each other or separated? In my father's house there was a plate with an illustration of two lovers divided by an angry sea. Does she dream about me like that, seeing me always away from her?

seven

•

DURING THE WEEK, there weren't many customers at the Empire. Reverend Duffy, though, came three or four times a week to eat a bucket of popcorn with no butter and watch whatever was playing. He especially liked the old mysteries, and to Jewel, who was pulling the drawer out of the cash register, it seemed fitting for a preacher to trace the clues in a whodunit as closely as he searches for the signs of his god. Seemed oddly fitting, too, that he spend so much time in an old dark movie house with an obelisk like a church spire and "GOD" painted in scarlet near the top. It was as if he realized god isn't something left by the Gideon Society, or the grand prize in Tuesday-night bingo bashes.

He had come to the Empire tonight because it was Friday. He would show up tomorrow night, too. On Sundays, he was in church all day, 8:30 and 10:30 for the Lutherans, 9:30 and 11:30 for the Episcopalians, and a 6:30 evening service for anybody else in the mood for it. She'd heard he was a good preacher and talked about movies a lot in his sermons. Jewel guessed that the movies were to him what the sermons were for the churchgoers: a few minutes being somewhere else, dreams coming true, no doubts about the bad guys, all those things that help people believe in something. Faith-growing sorts of things.

Jewel sighed and began counting the dollar bills. She imagined she had a thin layer of gray cinders covering her skin and hair. The extra weight had been there since early this afternoon, when she had started a fire in the wood stove. Weeks ago she had found some papers of no importance in her mother's room. Bills, junk mail, notes to herself, ordinary things Jewel had no use for. Burning them would not be a private moment, since fire could never be a private event. People would breathe in the scent of burning paper, recognizing the taste of it in their throats. Our private moment, Jewel decided, shifting the box of pages onto her lap, had been that moment of light in the kitchen. On the other hand, maybe there'd been no private moment at all, ever.

Swinging open the wood-stove door, she had shoved a handful of papers against the embers and watched as fire burst onto what was left of her mother's life. Up until I was seven years old, we always burned my letters to Santa Claus. I would sit at the kitchen table writing as neatly as I could a list of all the things I wanted for Christmas. It was never very long. Mama would have the wood stove burning so hot that if you were to spill water on the metal, the drops would dance into disappearing. She'd open the iron door and I would throw in my letter. The twists of yellow and red would melt every word even before the door slammed shut. Then we would rush outside to stare at the stovepipe. Do you see it, Jewel? Mama would ask, do you see it flying out with the fire? I would say, yes, I think so, though I was never sure what I was supposed to look for. And Mama would cry, there it is! There it goes!

Jewel stacked up the money from the night's take and put a rubber band around it. Sixty-eight dollars for both shows and concessions. Better than usual. But Mendez didn't care about the take, didn't even really care about the Empire except that it was his job. She couldn't blame him for his carelessness. Four years of college and three years of law school to end up being an errand boy for the Penhaligans.

Sometimes a shitty job is worth it, she decided, tossing the money into the bank bag and zipping it shut. Sometimes a job means being in the right place when love comes roaring up the street. Now that Dante has found me, I wake up with lust in my eyes, goodwill in my heart and a great desire to spout poetry. When I sneak out the front door of Mrs. Hilandera's boardinghouse to go home, my skin shimmers with the touch of her. Maybe tonight I'll stay till morning. Maybe tomorrow night. We can have Sunday breakfast at the Diamond Cafe, watching the church ladies on their way to service with their sensible shoes and strong hands. What Dante and I have been doing would shock the bejesus out of them. If they had a glimpse, just the slightest inkling, of this kind of joy, they'd fall right on the sidewalk with heart attacks, every one of them, their souls floating off to their respective makers.

Jewel used the word *makers* because she suspected that there were more than one. There were home gods and nature gods and gods of beer and Saturday nights, even a few car gods, though she didn't know if they were given that assignment on the basis of skill or the luck of the draw. There were gods of love and sex and gods of streets and rocking chairs. And gods of mobile homes, though she thought the jury was still out on whether her trailer was home for a god or a ghost.

As she tossed the bank deposit bag onto the shelf below the counter, a small beaded bracelet cascaded down her wrist. She didn't like jewelry as a rule, but she had clasped on the bracelet this morning. Her mother had made it. Necklaces, bracelets, chokers, she had strung the beads to keep her fingers busy. Yard-long pieces of silk had hung from the doorway of her mother's room, weighted with scissors, nail clippers, jars, anything her mother could loop a noose around. Jewel had plucked them off like strange fruit the day her mother died. Mama had said beads were better than TV, and reading gave her headaches. Maybe the bracelet was some proof of love, now that she was dead.

Stop, Jewel warned herself. It was never a question of love with Mama. Taking the key from its hiding place, she locked the register and candy counter. *Gaslight* was almost over, anybody wanting anything would just have to come back tomorrow. She'd turned off the popcorn machine in the middle of the second showing of *D.O.A.* and shoveled the leftovers into a plastic bag. Jewel glanced at the bracelet. I helped Mama die, what else did she ask of me? I came home every night, no matter how late, no matter how much I wanted to stay with someone else. I still come home every night, even though I know she's not there.

At first Jewel had thought it was habit, this compulsion. Her body was not yet used to the idea that her mother no longer needed someone to make sure she was breathing or to turn her over so she wouldn't get sores. But Jewel knew it was something else. Something dragged her away from the bed she was sharing with Dante or woke her to push her lover away. Dante never asked, she never even commented on it. It was as if she herself understood the pull of a familiar place. Maybe it was loving someone dead that she understood. It's easier to love dead people. Their goodness resonates and takes on a glow, while the bad is shaved away to a sliver, re-examined for greater meaning or simply forgotten.

Memory fails. Details that are loose to begin with fall away completely. It takes a great deal of energy to keep a dead woman sharp in your memory. Maybe that's what makes the dead easier to love—blunt edges don't hurt as much. So maybe that's what a ghost is, Jewel thought. The blurred outline with all the bad taken out. Or all the good. I don't know. Either way, I wonder if it is Mama's ghost that drags me back, her ghost or the gods of the place.

Where the hell was that girl? Jewel stepped around the counter and peered up the stairs. She'd seen Dante heading up to the projection booth with some pop and a box of Milk Duds for Donnie. Mostly she was going up to give him a pep talk—he was showing his movie tonight and had already almost started the place on fire when he threaded *D.O.A.* wrong. Nerves. Jewel would have sworn that after four years on the job, he could thread those projectors blindfolded, drunk and in a coma. Obviously not. She sighed and went back to her concession stand.

Dante was standing next to the projector nearest the projection-booth door watching Donnie pace. "Relax. It's only going to be us."

"I know, I know." He tilted the box of Milk Duds and let the last two roll into his mouth. Great, he thought. More sugar. Any more and I'm going to blast right through the roof of this place and into outer space. "I was thinking, maybe we could all go get a drink afterward, talk about it, what do you think?"

Dante shrugged and looked doubtful.

"I'll ask Jewel, see if she wants to go. We can get a couple of beers at the Mill." He tossed the empty candy box into a corner and continued pacing. Five steps, turn, five steps, turn, he walked the narrow aisle between the projectors and the back wall. Lacing his fingers, he pressed his palms tightly together.

"Seems like you could use a couple of drinks right now."

He smiled at her. "Yeah. It's just important to me. I mean, yeah, I'm nervous, but I'm worried nobody will understand what I'm doing."

"Maybe we won't. But you got to give us a chance, right? Who's going to be here?"

"Just you and Jewel and Turk."

Turk, Donnie James's creepy friend who wore sunglasses even at night and smelled like beer spilled on the floor of the backseat of a car, had swaggered up to the ticket window two flights below. He was orange from spending time in tanning booths, the tinge more like stage makeup than any color of skin, Jewel decided.

"Hey, babe," he said. "Donnie around?"

Jewel twitched her shoulder, her face wrinkling the tiniest bit as if she'd smelled something terrible but didn't want to mention it. "In the projection booth."

He flashed his teeth in a grin that made her want to dump ice down his back. "How about a beer after Donnie's movie, baby?"

"Get lost, George."

"Fuck you, bitch," he spat, walking into the theater.

Jewel watched as he strutted over to the stairs. He was wearing a black satin jacket with a dragon embroidered on the back and just above it, KOREA was stitched in the same gold thread as the flames coming from the creature's mouth. She closed her left eye as if aiming. Right in the dragon's eye. Just one little bullet and that would take care of him. She blinked and looked away. Would I shoot him? Yes. Go to jail? Yes. You don't break rules without facing the consequences.

Dante glanced out the small projectionist's window. She could see the outlines of heads and shoulders. There was Duffy in his usual seat to the far left because he preferred an elongated view. She could see a part of his face in the reflected light. His hand came up to his mouth and he chewed his popcorn steadily as if his eyes needed constant fueling.

Ingrid Bergman's beautiful face filled the screen. Dante smiled softly, then looked back at Duffy. His eyes hadn't moved, none of him had moved but that hand feeding popcorn into his mouth. She blinked, the smile dropping away. Is that what we're becoming? she wondered. Have movies started us down a path that will make human beings big-eyed creatures sitting in the darkness?

"Gaslight is almost over," Donnie announced, no longer pacing. "Like I was saying, Turk's okay, I mean, he used to be in the army but it didn't hurt him too bad."

Dante heard him clearly over the sound of the projector, but could not turn away from the outline of Reverend Duffy in the darkness. Will we evolve into thin-legged animals with eyes so large we don't have the room for taste or smell or the sense of touch?

"Can I ask you something, Dante?"

Dante turned quickly from the window to face him. "Sure."

"What's under that eye patch?"

"You want a look?" She lifted her hand and brushed the black velvet with her fingertips.

He turned away. Guess that's a no, she decided, running a finger along the edge of the eye patch, then dropping her hand. Duffy, the movies, metaphor; has the mind become an eye, seeking pictures in which to inject meaning? What happens to a one-eyed woman in a world full of pictures?

Donnie stood at the other projector, which had his film already threaded through its guts, and began fiddling with the knobs. "What happened?"

"What?" Dante looked at his shoulders. Donnie had tied back his wavy black hair and a little curl hung over his collar. Looks like a pigtail with ambitions, she thought. The black-and-white plaid of his shirt was tight across his back and tapered to a V at his waist. The flannel must be too warm for the little room. Her sweatshirt certainly was. She could feel a patch of sweat the size of her palm between her shoulder blades.

"What happened to your eye?" he called out, a little louder than was necessary.

"They say when Emperor Frederick II was a baby in the cradle, a rooster pecked out his eye and ate it in one gulp."

Donnie's shoulders tightened at the thought. She watched him nervously roll up his sleeves to the elbows. I guess I didn't really need to tell him that, she decided, walking over to the counter and leaning against it. Wedging her hands behind her back, Dante could feel the fringe of her hair against her wrists. "I lost my eye in an accident."

"What kind of accident?" Donnie stopped messing with the projector and looked at her over his shoulder.

"One minute I had my eye, the next, half the world went dark. That kind of accident." She pushed away from the counter. "I'm going downstairs. Jewel said something about making the bank deposit early so we wouldn't have to wait for your movie to start."

Dante ducked out of the room and slowly walked down the stairs. What happens to a one-eyed woman? She let one hand glide down the railing and felt herself starting a long slide into sadness. Maybe the change in temperature or the moldy smell of the stairs and walls, maybe the Empire itself leaning on her with its age made her eye start to tear and the skin and nerves of her missing eye itch. She tapped the patch with one hand to stop the tingling. Flicking her finger at the velvet made a hollow, flat sound, like a drum with the head too loose.

We shall see what will happen to me, she thought, running her hand along the faded velvet curtain of one of the windows on the landing. The curtains were never closed, just held back by gold tassels that looked brassy green in the light. Dante was partial to velvet. In addition to the black velvet eye patch over her left eye, she had a dark-green one with her initials embroidered in the lower corner and another black one with a Japanese character for thank you stitched on it. There are more than five ways to say thank you in Japanese, and each one has a varying degree of resentment built into it. People in Japan recognize that to be grateful is a kind of slavery, she thought.

Dante had wanted a traditional drawing of a scorpion that she had seen on the wall of a tattoo shop in Banjarmasin. It was like a knife with no handle, only blades curving out dangerously in many directions, solid black and slightly evil. There was no mistaking this scorpion for a benign astrological symbol or a good-luck charm. It was the sinisterness of the scorpion that made her select the Japanese ideogram; her lost eye was not something malignant.

People began straggling out of the auditorium, shuffling into their coats. Reverend Duffy walked slowly into the lobby, his black overcoat over his arm. At least, Jewel thought, putting away the glass cleaner and rag she'd used to polish the candy counter, if she didn't like Duffy's preaching, she could appreciate his film criticism. He always found something new, no matter how many times he'd seen the movie.

He was shaking his head, his silvery hair catching the light. "Yes, I'm quite sure now. *Film noir* started it all."

"Started what?"

"Directors started making movies filled with doubt. Before that you knew just by looking who was bad and who was good." He shook out his coat. "One look at Scarface and you knew there was going to be trouble. One grin from Carole Lombard and you knew everything would be all right. Now all the outsides have changed, like a strange jigsaw puzzle whose pieces don't picture anything no matter how many times you take them apart and put them together. What happened? Used to be we were all wanting to ride off into the sunset. Now all we want is to argue with god, show pimples on an ugly man's back and put stars under a microscope."

"Something wrong with not wanting to ride off into the sunset?"

"I don't know." Duffy pulled on the coat and began buttoning it. "But I should know by now the effect *film noir* has on me, Jewel. It just reminds me that there is no more simple faith."

"Or no more faith of the simple. Maybe people get more complicated as time goes by."

"Maybe." He put his fedora on his head, raked at an angle she knew he copied from Bogart in *The Maltese Falcon*. "So much doubt, you know. These movies are filled with doubt and dread."

"You have to admit that doubt and dread can be pretty interesting."

"Sometimes." Duffy took a step away, then stopped to look back at her. "I just found out I will be having a young man staying in the rectory with me, a divinity student. Only this young man used to be a young woman."

Jewel's eyebrows went up, then down. "A transvestite preacher? Now there's a story for you."

"Transsexual, Jewel. He is a transsexual. I've done some reading, but can books ever prepare you for the real thing?" He shook his head slowly and buckled the belt of his coat with his thick fingers. "This world is moving so fast."

She watched Franklin Duffy leave the theater, his shoulders hunched against the rain. He walked slowly down the sidewalk, then turned into a blurry outline against the streetlight outside the cafe. A man dressed in black can disappear easily on a night like this, she thought, coming back to the front counter. Maybe that's what I need, to be able to disappear. Just for a while. Disappear, and return with a grin. If anyone asks, I'd say I went to visit a friend. A friend who lives in the mountains. Someone living alone. Someone lonely.

"You like him, don't you?"

"Who? Reverend Duffy? Sure. Why not?" Jewel took her jacket from the shelf. "Where have you been?"

"Upstairs keeping Donnie calm. He's scared shitless."

"He's always scared shitless."

Dante glanced up at the stairs as if expecting him to come bouncing down. "He likes you a lot."

"What's not to like?" She flashed her heartbreaking smile.

"I mean, he really likes you."

"I know that."

"You don't feel anything for him?"

Jewel pulled on her jacket. "Sorry enough to pose for a painting last summer, but not so sorry that I'd do it again."

"Why not?"

"He stood there with a brush in his hand and a stiffy in his pants. Didn't excuse himself, didn't drop a bucketful of ice down his drawers to calm down, nothing. The whole time I was sitting there in my shorts and T-shirt, I could see it pushing out his jeans like a tent pole."

Dante watched Jewel tug her hair out of her collar and had the sudden desire to touch her lover's face. "Sounds like a compliment. You weren't flattered?"

"I only enjoy sexual flattery from people I find sexually attractive."

"So if I say I think you have great tits—"

"I'm glad I've made myself understood."

There was a heartbeat moment when they both leaned toward each other. Then Jewel grinned again and pulled back.

"See," she continued, glancing from Dante's mouth to her eye, "Donnie James Champlin is not a turn-on. If sex were a grocery store, he would be the frozen food section."

"I get it."

Jewel leaned on the counter. "Don't get me wrong, I like him well enough. I hope this movie thing works out, I hope he gets somewhere with his painting, but he's got no, I don't know, whatever it is that makes an artist out of somebody."

"What is that? What makes an artist out of somebody?"

"Fire. Passion. The same thing that makes a good lover." Jewel studied Dante's face for a moment. "What would you say if we skipped—"

Just then, a young woman and a young man stepped up to the counter.

"Alma, Antone, how are you two doing?" Jewel asked.

"We're all right," the young woman answered. "Me and Antone want to ask you about the trailer, you know, if you've decided when we can move in."

Jewel put her hands on her hips. "Steve mentioned it on the phone this afternoon."

Alma leaned against the glass counter, both hands clutching her purse. Dante glanced at the thin gold band on her left hand, then at her cuff and up the sleeve of her jacket to her face. She and Jewel could almost be sisters, she thought. Same mouth, same hair. As Alma talked, Dante concentrated on the small beauty mark above her lip. She looked at Antone, who had one arm around Alma's waist and his other hand stuffed in his jeans pocket, then back at her. What a lovely woman, but both of them are too young for marriage and setting up a house.

"How about Sunday?" Jewel asked, brushing her hair out of her face with one hand. "I'll get rid of my boxes in the morning and you can move in that afternoon."

Dante noticed the small bead bracelet slip down Jewel's wrist, then looked at Antone again. He managed his father's gas station and had a 1968 Kawasaki parked in back that he rolled into the garage to tinker with when he had the chance. He'd been the one to tell her about Mrs. Hilandera's boardinghouse, after walking around her Harley a couple of times and letting out a long, low whistle.

"How's it going?" Dante asked him casually.

"It's going," he answered.

"How's the bike?"

"All right. Still at the gas station." He gave her a friendly grin. "Too cold to ride, anyway."

"Never too cold."

Alma looked from Dante to Antone and back to Jewel. "You call me when you're out of there," she said to Jewel.

"I will."

"Come on, Antone," she said, putting her hand on his at her waist and leading him to the door.

"Pretty woman," Dante said, watching them disappear in the darkness.

"Think so?"

"Yeah. Now, what were you going to say?"

"Forget it." Jewel grabbed the deposit bag from under the counter. "I have to get to the bank."

"You want me to go with you?"

"No, that's okay. I'll be fine, darling. Tell Donnie I'll be back— don't start without me." As Jewel walked behind her, she brushed Dante's hip with her hand. "Tonight?"

"Yes."

Jewel smiled and walked toward the door, pulling it open just as another woman stepped in.

"God, what a night," the woman exclaimed. She looked past Jewel at Dante. "Where's Donnie? I'm here to see the movie."

Jewel stared at the woman, then spoke to Dante. "I'll be back in a minute."

The glass door shut behind her. Jewel looked both ways and crossed the street, careful to step over the larger cracks in the road. She walked between two halos of light from the street lamps, leaving them behind with every step. Jewel liked the darkness. She liked being able to hide in it. Sometimes I think that's what my life is, she thought. Circling around and around to find the best way to become inconspicuous.

Dante studied the woman standing in the doorway of the Empire. Her hair, brushed up and sprayed, was as brown as the rain spots on the shoulders of her suede coat. Her face was oval, her earrings were square and the blue shoes she was wearing had little white triangles on the toes. She's my age, Dante thought, but my god how different we are. I'll get old and fall off my motorcycle; she'll get old and fall to pieces. It already shows in her face.

"Well?"

"Donnie's in the booth. Go up both flights of stairs and keep going left."

"I know where it is."

"Do you want a candy bar or something? Popcorn? Got a whole bag of it."

"No." The woman slid her jacket off. "Thank you anyway."

She left Dante alone, leaning against the glass counter. Dante peered across the street looking for a sign of Jewel. The darkness outside seemed to push her vision back inside, to settle on the cherubs fluttering in every corner of the lobby. What kind of an artist could really believe such fat angels could fly with such little wings? Ugly as they are, at least they're well lighted. Is that what people want, to be anywhere as long as it isn't in the dark? She glanced around the small concession stand. The pop dispenser, popcorn machine, the candy counters, all of them have lights. Maybe it isn't just to get people's attention. Maybe we got all this brightness to reassure one another. Dante shook her head and glanced at the stairs. Hope Donnie's ready.

Sue Potts stood in the doorway of the projection booth.

"Hey, Sue," Turk said, scrambling from the floor to his feet.

"Sue?" Donnie looked up from the projector. "I didn't know you were going to be here."

"Turk told me about it."

"Glad you could make it." Turk shoved his hands into the back pockets of his jeans.

"So that's the weird skinny girl with the eye patch. Everybody's talking about her."

"She's all right. Her name's Dante."

"Is she foreign?"

"She's from back East."

"License plate says Connecticut," Turk offered.

"Huh. Wonder what she did to get the job."

"She was in the right place at the right time. Jewel put in a good word for her." Donnie said, putting the last reel of *Gaslight* into a slot below the splicing table.

"I bet." Turk leered. "Everybody knows how good Jewel is with her mouth."

"Shut up, Turk." Donnie's voice had an edge in it.

"Right, right." Turk slid down the wall. "Hey, did you hear Cindy Frizano is pregnant?"

Sue laid her purse and jacket on the back counter. "And she doesn't know who the father is."

"She's so skinny, she's going to look like a flagpole with a bowling ball stuck to it."

Sue Potts giggled and pulled out a cigarette.

"Don't smoke," Donnie shot out.

"Why not?"

"It's hot and stuffy enough as it is."

"You wouldn't say that if this was a joint."

"That's true," Turk stuck in.

"Just don't, okay?"

"God, what is happening to you? You're beginning to act like an old man."

"He's not getting any younger."

"And if you want to get any older, you'll shut up."

Donnie's friends watched him in amazement. He wiped the sweat off his forehead. "I'm sorry. I don't know what's the matter with me."

"If I didn't know any better, I'd say you had one hell of a case of PMS. Look at those boxes of Milk Duds." Sue pointed to the corner where the six empties lay in a heap.

"Don't be nervous, Donnie. We got faith in you."

"Thanks, buddy." Donnie smiled at the man sitting on the floor. He could be such a pain in the ass, but when you needed a push, Turk was always right there.

"Hey," Turk continued. "We're going to have a job opening at the animal shelter. You interested?"

"Doing what? Cleaning cages?" Sue asked.

"Animal Control Assistant. What do you think?"

"That's great, George. Donnie can go from being a projector to a dog catcher. What a step up in the world."

"I'm not a projector," Donnie said quietly and pointed to a machine. "That's a projector. I'm a projectionist."

"It's civil service," Turk said. "Good benefits. Pay isn't so hot at first, but if you stick around long enough to get a desk job, it gets pretty good."

"I don't know, Turk."

"You'll be serving the community."

Sue laughed. "Doing what? Protecting us from squirrels and French poodles?"

"I've had hassles with some pretty dangerous animals, Sue."

"Yeah. Like guinea pigs and baby deer."

"I had to capture a Doberman, a trained attack dog. He turned on his master."

"Do they really do that?"

"You bet," Turk answered, nodding quickly. "See, their brains grow too big. After a while, they start pushing on their skulls and that turns them vicious."

Donnie rolled his eyes. "What he's not telling you is that twenty other people went after that dog. He stayed in the truck."

"I was in charge of communications. Even if Dobermans don't kill you they can rip your arm off. Mean motherfuckers."

"Right." Donnie shrugged. "Why don't you get Jewel and Dante and find some seats?"

Sue Potts put the unlit cigarette between her lips and lifted her lighter. "Jewel was leaving just as I came in."

Jewel held the front of her jacket closed with one hand and walked quickly to the bank. Sue Potts. There was something obscene about Sue Potts. She was too clean and too goody-goody. I'd like to spit on both my hands and mess up her hair, she thought. Sue Potts doesn't like to come to the Empire, not if it meant associating with the town whore, as if she isn't running a close second. She just keeps it hidden, while I take refuge in a sure reputation. Because people have decided they know me, my life goes unexamined from now on. Especially with Mama gone.

Jewel pulled in a lungful of fresh air. It tasted damp. Thank god for the rain, she thought. Mama hadn't liked rain, it kept her indoors. One ray of sunshine and she'd be outside, even when she was sick. After I'd go to work and before the duty nurse would arrive, Mama would crawl from her bedroom, down the narrow hall past the bathroom, through the kitchen, out the front door and plop into an old office chair we kept behind the mobile-home skirting. I should've known she had a reason other than wanting to sit in the sun, but what could she possibly do with that old chair?

She rode it, that's what she did. Though most of the stuffing had escaped out of the long tears in the seat and the back, the rusted wheels could still roll.

The liquor store had stopped delivering, but Carl Frizano had no twinges of guilt about selling to Mama face to face. A bottle of scotch on her lap and back she'd come, pulling herself with her heels. A block there, a block back, the sidewalks broken and covered with trash, and Mama would make it back before the nurse showed up. People who knew Mama shouldn't have been drinking would help her, pushing the chair, loosening a wheel that got caught or clearing something out of the way.

"Dante?" Donnie yelled from the top of the stairs.

She turned from the counter and yelled back, "Yeah?"

"Did Jewel leave?"

"Went to make the bank deposit."

Donnie walked back into the booth, his eyebrows knitted together. Jewel's got to see my film. I did it for her. "It's all right. Jewel just went to make the deposit. She's got to do it since Mendez only comes by once a week."

"That's a fucking weird situation with Mendez and the Penhaligans. Where is Virgil, anyway?"

"I don't know. It's hard to tell." Donnie glanced out the nearest projection window into the theater. "He's not sweeping out the seats yet. Might be cleaning the bathrooms. Hey, guess what I found out about Virgil Nut Case Penhaligan."

"What?" they asked in unison.

"He's got a hole in the wall of the women's bathroom so he can look in."

"That's gross!" Sue cried.

Turk was laughing. "That's great. He gets his rocks off watching them pee?"

"Bet he does."

"Bet he doesn't know what to do with a woman, anyway,"

Turk snorted, picking at his ear. "Some kind of bad luck, him having all that money and not knowing what to do with it. Fucking psycho waiting to go off, if you ask me."

"Nobody asked you, Turk," Sue cut in.

"Shit, what's this?" Turk said in surprise. "You defending Virgil? What did you do, fuck him or something?"

"I'd never fuck a dead man come back to life." She smiled at Donnie and took a deep drag of her cigarette.

Donnie sighed. Women. What was the use of telling them anything? "Turk, block open the door, would you? Use the fire extinguisher."

"Sure." Turk knocked over the small red extinguisher twice before setting it in place. "How long before show time?"

Donnie shrugged.

"You going to show this anywhere else? They got film festivals all over the place where you could enter it. Los Angeles, New York—imagine Donnie James Champlin winning some hot-shit prize at Cannes."

Donnie smiled. "Be something, wouldn't it?"

"You'd have to go to Europe. To the Mediterranean. Topless beaches there, man. Me, I'd go with you in a New York minute."

"Me, too. I'd love to live near the ocean," Sue said, crossing her arms. "Where does your ex-wife live?"

"Coos Bay."

"Supposed to be real pretty there. You ever been?"

"No, haven't been anywhere. Bend, Portland—went to Seattle once."

"Man, that's pathetic. Thirty years old and the only place you've ever been is Bend-over, Oregon. You should get some traveling done, now that you're a free man."

Donnie glanced at the power box, double-checking the prelight switch for the left projector. "Dante's been everywhere. Russia. China."

"I've been to Japan." Turk tugged on his jacket. "When I was stationed in Korea I went all over the place. You know they eat dogs over there in the Orient."

"You always say that."

"Slants will eat anything."

"Shut up with the racist crap, would you? You sound even more ignorant than you are."

"It's true, Donnie. They'll eat anything, even your little brother."

"I don't have a little brother."

"If you did, they'd throw him in the oven and turn him into teriyaki. Trust me, you don't want to go there."

"Going somewhere is better than going nowhere," Sue stuck in.

"You said it, honey," Donnie agreed. "And I don't want to be going nowhere."

Turk shook his head. "With your talent? You're going to set the world on fire and I mean that. Maybe some studio will want you to direct something. You could shoot on location anywhere you'd want."

"I wouldn't mind going to the Bahamas," Sue said. "It's warm there, like Mazatlán."

Donnie shook his head, grinned at her and looked back at Turk. "People don't let you make movies after seeing one thing. Especially not after seeing this—it's experimental."

Sue cocked her head and looked at him out of one eye. "What does that mean?"

"Well—" Donnie stopped short. "You just have to see it, that's all."

Jewel stepped on the curb and walked slowly to the glass doors of the theater. Dante was waiting at the counter. She was watching me, Jewel realized. Watching me go over to the bank and back. A drop of rain slid past her right eye and down her cheek.

"Glad to see you back," Dante said softly, holding open the door.

"Is Sue Potts staying for Donnie's movie?"

"You mean the woman with the big hair? I suppose so."

"Sue Potts is a Barbie doll."

"I had a Barbie doll when I was little, only I shaved off all her hair and made her drive a Tonka truck."

"I believe it," Jewel said, unable to move her eyes from Dante's lips. She has a wonderful mouth, Jewel decided, wanting to kiss her slowly and carefully for the next hundred years or so. She followed the line of Dante's face up her cheekbones to her eye. The iris was a paler blue toward the center than on the outside, her lashes long, her eyebrows straight and very dark. Jewel's fingers itched for a moment. I want to touch her. I want to kiss and bite and tumble together.

"What are we waiting for?" Dante asked quietly.

"I want to brush my hair first."

Dante grinned at her. "Hurry up. The sooner we see this, the sooner we leave."

Donnie peered out the projectionist's window again. Dante was walking slowly toward the screen to open the curtain and turn down the lights. Jewel must be back. For a moment, he wanted to race down the stairs to check. Get a hold of yourself, he commanded, shoving his hands into his back pockets, then his front pockets, finally giving up and crossing his arms.

Sue looked at Turk, sitting on the floor. "Why don't you get us some seats? I'd like to talk to Donnie alone."

"Yeah, sure." Turk got back to his feet. "You want me to save one for you, Donnie, or are you going to stay up here?"

"I'm staying here."

Sue closed the door behind Turk and turned to face Donnie. "I just wanted to say that I really enjoyed last night."

She crossed the small room and slid her arms around his neck. "And I also wanted to say that I think you're very brave for showing your movie. I'd never have the guts."

Donnie kissed her lightly. "Thanks, Sue. That really means a lot to me."

"I'll be downstairs, waiting for you."

She left the projection booth. Donnie was alone and the room was charged with the sound of rain, its scattered sound hushing everything for a moment. He glanced down at the main floor. Dante was standing in the aisle, waving up at him. He waved, too, and glanced around the main floor. Jewel must be in the bathroom.

Jewel watched the reflection of Sue Potts triple her chin in order to rouge her cleavage. As if anyone really cares what color her tits are, Jewel thought, brushing her hair back from her face. Keeping her elbows close to her sides since there wasn't much room in front of the mirror, Jewel loosened a tangle of hair with her fingers and kept brushing. I wish Dante was doing this, she thought, the idea causing a small ache between her breasts. I love her. I want her. The way people act, you'd think that to admit I love Dante would cause the world to be tossed into chaos: Ships would sink, trains derail and every window in the world shatter.

Donnie stared out the projectionist's window. Sue sat down next to Turk and they both stared up at him, their faces like playing cards—all outline and primary colors. As the houselights began to dim, Sue waved. Donnie raised his hand, but she had already turned to the screen.

Dante let go of the dimmer and began pulling the curtain rope hand over hand. The hemp was soft to touch, without the bite of new rope. The stage smelled like dust and camphor, and the pulleys seemed to groan with effort. Age, Dante realized. The metal wheels sound like old age.

Where is Jewel? Donnie wondered. He shifted his weight from foot to foot and crossed his arms. There, across the aisle from Turk and Sue. Dante would be out in a minute, as soon as she finished opening the curtain. He blinked, wiped the sweat from his eyes, then threw the motor switch. His film began clicking through the projector, and he turned the focusing ring of the lens till the numbers on the screen were sharp. Five seconds and it all begins.

eight

•

JEWEL HAD NOTICED that when there was music playing in the theater, everyone talked louder. It had nothing to do with being heard. Classical music hushed people, made them speak in low tones that carried through the sound of the strings and French horns. Rock made people shout and throw their Goobers at each other. Jazz, even bad jazz, made the room seem smaller, the ceiling lower, and seemed to blend with conversation at the counterpoint. Silence, however, built a tension in the room, almost a wall between the people and the screen. Rain made the silence bigger, heavier, making you afraid to laugh or even zip your jacket for fear of being conspicuous.

Dante skipped down the stairs stage left toward Turk, Sue and Jewel, who were standing in the aisle not looking at one another. Dante had left the houselights up at less than half, as she always did at the end of the evening's show. On her first night, she had noticed that the light fixtures on the main floor were the same angels as in the lobby, but the chrome was chipping off them. It was an odd effect, as if these gleaming figures had a case of leprosy attacking their faces, wings and bodies. She doubted there were plans to replace them; Virgil would just keep rotating the worst ones into the darkest areas till none of the fixtures had any chrome left at all. Where is Virgil, anyway? she wondered, joining the others as Donnie came hurrying down the aisle.

"Well?" Donnie broke into the silence.

"I'd really like a drink," Sue Potts said, snapping her purse open and shut, then flipping the strap onto her shoulder.

"Sounds good to me," Turk said. "Jewel, how about you and your friend there?"

"I don't think so."

"Would you quit talking about nothing and tell me what you thought? Somebody? Anybody?" Donnie cried, an edge of panic in his voice. The sound of the rain outside closed around them like a velvet curtain. Every now and then there was a sharp *ping* as a drop hit an air vent or the rain gutters. He saw Dante shoot a look at Jewel, an exchange as fast as a machete dismembering a hand. "Dante?"

"Umm," Dante rubbed her face for a moment. "I thought you had some pretty good ideas going. Some of the juxtaposition of images was all right. I liked the shots from *Casablanca,* but that's one of my favorite old flicks."

Sue looked behind Turk at Dante. Her mouth was open in disbelief. "What's a juxtaposition?"

"The way he put one hunk of movie next to another," Turk answered.

"Oh. Yeah, I thought that was really good, too. How come it was all black-and-white?"

"That's all the film I had," Donnie explained, glancing at Jewel. Baby? Won't you say anything?

"I thought the black-and-white looked good." Turk nodded enthusiastically. "You know, sort of, uh, basic. Like some of those pen-and-ink drawings you have. People are supposed to focus on form and the way one set of shapes goes with another, right?"

"Yeah. I was really trying to get a new way for people to see a movie. We expect movies to somehow have a context, with images flowing in a linear form. The way conversations are supposed to. When they made those old movies everything was controlled— each thread in the costumes, every word, every reaction. I wanted to kind of blow that out of your minds. I wanted to mess with your sense of time and context."

Jewel peeked at Dante from the corner of her eye, then looked back to Donnie. I wonder if he got that out of a book or if he's making it up as he goes along, she thought.

"Donnie?" Dante asked, hesitant. "Did you watch this before showing it to us?"

"Nope," he said proudly. "I wanted it to happen to me like it would to you."

"What did you think?"

Donnie ran his hand through his hair. "A little disjointed. There's so much movement without anything to hang on to."

"A lack of context," Turk muttered, stroking his chin with his fingers.

"How did you create the film?" Dante continued.

"Piled all the clips I had, pulled them out of a bag one at a time. I just stuck them together. The only thing I did was put everything right side up. At first I was going to connect the pieces by shared elements. Like everything with water in it would go together, all the scenes with one guy or two guys, kind of match it all up."

"Like playing cards," Sue said suddenly.

"Kind of," Donnie hurried on. "But then I saw I was just going along with this human trait of grouping things. And that's what I was trying to fight against, you know?"

"Achieving some kind of purposeful chaos?" Dante asked, her face blank and her eyebrows lifted.

"Yeah. That's it. Right. Exactly. Trying to examine purposeful chaos. Putting all these pictures together in the way that stuff happens every day." He was looking at Jewel directly now. "The arbitrariness in life can sometimes bring about meaningful coincidence."

"Synchronicity?" Dante suggested.

"Fate?" Jewel asked, turning to Dante. "Destiny?"

Dante nodded. Please, Jewel, she begged. Please say something. The poor guy is going to fall down at your feet and beg for you to spit on him just to get a response.

"Some people call that kismet, don't they?" Jewel continued, still talking to Dante.

"Do you believe in those things, Donnie?" Dante asked, hoping to push Jewel's attention to him.

"I believe some things are bound to come together. They can't escape one another. It's a special kind of magnetism." Donnie stared at Jewel. He felt his strength burning away like lightning hitting the ground.

"Maybe a special kind of gravity," Dante said softly. "Is that what faith is?"

" 'Is that what faith is?' " he echoed, surprised. "I don't know."

"You know, I think you got something," Turk said, nodding his head at Dante. "Maybe Donnie's film is about how, you know, religion and faith is so pointless and empty. You know, how man wants to believe in order to make himself feel important."

"Maybe man does," Dante said, fighting the urge to elbow Jewel in the ribs. "But I don't think women do."

"Oh, okay, all right. I meant man to mean everybody."

"I know you did. But it doesn't." Donnie, don't stare at Jewel, Dante thought. She isn't going to give you what you're looking for. She's not going to give you anything. "Donnie, do you think faith is a special kind of gravity?"

"Maybe." Please, Jewel, tell me. He blinked, feeling dizzy. Too much sugar, too much tension. "What did you think of my movie, Jewel?"

"It was fine."

"Really? Is that what you really think?"

"It was okay, Donnie."

"You can tell me, I can take it."

Jewel sighed. She had wanted to like it. But after the first three seconds, her stomach had lurched, as if she were in an elevator that was dropping too quickly. Let it get better, please, she had prayed. I want to like him and I want to like this. One more bad attempt will earn him only my pity.

"Come on, Jewel."

She unfolded her jacket and stuck her arms into the sleeves. "It was terrible."

"It was not," Sue Potts interjected.

"Your movie wasn't about life being pointless. It was pointless." Her expression hammered each word into him like a nail.

"That's shit," Turk growled. "You know dick about art."

Jewel ignored him and stared at Donnie.

"I was just trying to do something new."

"And you're too stupid to see that," Turk sneered.

"Actually, the idea isn't new." Dante's voice was quiet. "A man named Bruce Connor spliced together bits from old films, very similar to what you did, Donnie. He made a classic experimental film called *A Movie*."

"Really?" Donnie asked, his voice just above a whisper.

"Really. But that doesn't mean your film is worthless."

"Hell, no," Turk butted in.

"But Jewel thinks so," Donnie replied.

"Yeah, I guess I do." Pushing her way past, Jewel walked up the aisle to the door.

Donnie looks like he's been kicked in the nuts, Dante thought. I can't believe he was counting on her so much.

"What a bitch," Turk muttered.

"Shut up, Turk," Donnie responded automatically.

Dante stepped between Donnie and Sue. She studied him for a moment. It's like he's hiding that he's gasping for air, for every single breath. Reaching across the space between them, she touched Donnie's arm below the roll of his sleeve. His skin was warm, and the black hairs were like lines someone had drawn on him, wavy and matted down. Her fingers were perpendicular to the line of his arm, intersecting softly just above his wrist. "I'll see you tomorrow."

"Yeah. Tomorrow."

Dante followed Jewel slowly up the aisle, pulling on her jacket. The leather was cool in the still, stale air of the Empire, and it felt slick on her hands when she pulled the collar up. It didn't smell much like leather anymore, she realized as she stepped into the lobby. Cigarettes, the scent from her own body, the odor of gasoline, they were all there like an invisible cocoon against the smell of decay and stale popcorn of the theater. Crossing the lobby to Jewel, she noticed Virgil, washing the tall window on the landing that looked out on the parking lot.

"Good night, Virgil," she called as she and Jewel stepped out of the theater.

Virgil wiped the glass in a circle. He had seen them watching something he didn't recognize. He'd spied on that girl with the one eye and the funny name as she brought down the lights. From behind the curtain, he could see where they were sitting in the darkness: five rows back, center aisle, on the right. Best seats in the house, he'd always thought. The man with the sunglasses and the girl with the big hair were sitting on one side of the aisle, Jewel and the one-eyed girl on the other.

The hinges of the auditorium door squeaked as it banged open. "Don't worry about it." A man's voice drifted up the stairs. "Jewel Mraz doesn't know anything, I'm telling you, Donnie."

Donnie James Champlin, the girl with the hair and the skinny man. Virgil watched them as they walked to the doors.

"Just a second." Donnie walked to the middle of the lobby. "Virgil?"

Virgil pulled the rag away from the window and stepped down onto the top stair.

"Virgil?" Donnie called again, a little louder. Where is that fuckhead? "Virgil!"

Virgil took another step down, his weight making the stair creak. Donnie looked up to see Virgil's feet. "I'm leaving. I'll lock the door behind me. Everybody's gone but you, okay?"

Without waiting for a response, Donnie turned back to his friends. His keys rattled an ugly chime against the glass, then Virgil was alone.

He stood on the second stair for a moment, listening to the hush of the empty theater. Carefully, as if the steps would cave in beneath him, he walked the rest of the way down, through the auditorium door and down the center aisle. Fifth row from the front, Virgil thought. The one-eyed girl had been closest to the aisle in the first seat, and Jewel in the second. He stopped and peered around the theater, polishing an arm rest. Never know who might be spying on him. He stepped quickly down the row and perched on the third seat, the better to examine where Jewel had been.

The cushion was tearing at the corners and small threads hung where the fabric stopped and the metal started. He stared at a small burn. It was almost a perfect circle, as if someone had held the end of a cigarette against it. Virgil poked his finger into it, the red weave giving easily, and enlarged the hole. Firetrap. Place is a firetrap, in spite of the rain. Flattening his hand, he pushed the seat down, leaving his palm against the rough fabric. There was a hollow where so many people had sat over the years. Virgil could feel where the stuffing had been crushed down. The spring still worked; the seat kept wanting to return upright. He raised his hand a little and the cushion followed.

She was here, he thought. Virgil squeezed his eyes shut. The dream from last night began playing in his head, as if it were a movie showing against the back of his eyelids. He could see Jewel's bare breasts coming toward him, then her thighs, open. Though he couldn't see her face, he knew it was her, knew that the body belonged to her, that it was Temptation; the Devil himself had searched Virgil's soul and brain for his weakest point and had given him this. Jewel. His Temptation. He had sat in his narrow bed, his hand crushing the stained sheet, his face becoming wet with tears. I've failed. I have succumbed. The despair echoed over and over like a promise of doom. He was not Special. He was caught, caught like every man on earth in the clutches of such Sin. The beauty he had once rejoiced in had betrayed him, had almost destroyed him. He could see it all so clearly, there in the night. He knew that was Hell—to see with absolute, pain-filled clarity even in pitch darkness.

Now, sitting in the Empire, Virgil felt like a small, incredibly ugly insect. How quick his defeat had been. How difficult his return to purity. It was the stealing that had caught him. Her comb in the pocket of his overalls. His right hand still on the theater seat, he placed his left hand on the stitched bib covering his chest. The comb was still there. Penance was due. Prayer and more prayer. Here. At the site of the Sin.

nine

•

JEWEL SCORNED THE film he had spent so much time creating. The images he had spliced, cut and respliced. Donnie could feel the slow crush of humiliation in his stomach, his face burning with the memory. He felt his jaw clench, biting down hard on something he couldn't crush or release. Who cared what Dante said? What did she know? She wasn't an artist. And she wasn't the woman he loved. Jewel knew. She had been right. It wasn't good enough. His work would never be good enough until she approved. Until he saw the gleam in her eyes when she recognized an accomplishment. When she saw his talent and discipline. It was all he could offer her. It was how he would win her. With paintings, with creation, with the very essence of himself spread across canvas in the portrait of her. He was painting his heart and he wouldn't fail this time.

God, what am I going to do about Sue Potts? She doesn't understand. She can't, she doesn't have the ability to go beyond her own tiny life. All she knows how to do is call people like Jewel names. Bitch, slut, whore—each word makes Sue's face a little uglier till I can barely stand to look at her. But it's so easy to be around her. She doesn't demand, doesn't push. All she wants is a good time, to spend the night sometimes, and to hear nice, easy compliments. But I don't love her. I'll never love her. My heart belongs to someone else, someone who broke it by letting it fall out of her grasp. And she doesn't even care. Jewel doesn't even care.

Donnie got out of bed and walked into the kitchen. Taking the binoculars out of the drawer, he held them to his eyes. No lights on at her mobile home. No sign of movement. She must have slipped in when he wasn't looking and was now sound asleep without a stain on her conscience. God, how could she hurt him? How could she hurt him and not even know it? Maybe she did know it. Maybe she could feel his pain. For the first time, he realized that he was attached to this world by a few slender threads that could break soundlessly with a change of emotion or position, and the strongest of the threads was the one tied to Jewel. Donnie dropped his hands, her window getting smaller in the distance. Maybe this was the price of loving her. Hurt. Anger. The spurs cutting him to work harder.

He crossed the dark room carefully. Maybe I should tell her, he thought. Maybe if she knew how much she hurt me. . . . His thoughts trailed off. That's what I have to do. I'll tell her. Donnie returned to his bed, sat on the edge and looked at the clock radio. It was almost four in the morning.

Dante woke up, surprised at the warmth surrounding her. Jewel. Jewel was keeping her warm. "You awake, darling?" Dante whispered, hoping she was sound asleep.

"Yeah," Jewel answered.

Dante pulled her closer. Jewel's hair smelled like a bonfire, a warm, comforting scent. In my father's house during winter, Dante thought, as soon as the edge of the roof was fixed with icicles, tiny teeth at the top of each window, he would build a fire in the fireplace, a huge roaring thing that made us sleepy with its heat. Why do I carry with me things that are useless in my everyday life, but that are still of him and from him? Why do I think about these things now? She breathed deeply, taking in the scent of her lover, then sat up to lean against the carved headboard. "I fell asleep."

"I know."

She stroked Jewel softly as if she were a flower—without desire now, but with a delicate nearness. She ran her hand over her lover's hip with an intimate knowledge. A beautiful woman is a delight.

"What time is it?"

Dante reached for the alarm clock, tilting the face toward the light coming in the window. "Almost four."

"What are you thinking about?"

"I was thinking how lovely you are," she said softly, setting the clock back on the nightstand. "How about you?"

"I was thinking of this clock that used to be in the living room at home. It had a ship on the end of its pendulum that rocked away every second. I gave it away right after my mom died and was just thinking how I wish I'd kept it."

Jewel sat up, leaning on her elbow to look at Dante's face. She wanted to keep talking, to tell Dante that sometimes she felt like that ship, swinging away hours and not getting anywhere. She wanted to tell her that there were times when she could almost see her mother watching as they made love, and that no matter what Jewel did, she couldn't escape. She wanted to explain that her mother's absence hissed like steam. Instead, she leaned over and kissed Dante's mouth.

"Will you stay? Mrs. Hilandera can throw me out if she wants."

"I doubt she would. She needs the money and as long as no one else complains, I'm sure she doesn't care." Jewel smiled and laid her head down. "I'd really like to, but I can't."

Dante wrapped her arms around her, then shifted deeper into the blankets. "Jewel?"

"Hmm?"

"What is Virgil's deal?"

"Virgil? He's crazy," Jewel said simply.

"Just because he's weird doesn't mean the elevator doesn't go to the top floor."

"He's crazy, really. He got struck by lightning and it burned up his brain."

"What?"

"He got struck by lightning when he was a kid. He was all by himself when he got hit. The lightning popped him wide open; he's got a big white scar all the way down his spine from where his skin split open. His heart stopped for four minutes while he was in the emergency room."

"No way."

Jewel sat up again, leaving Dante's arms. "Yes way. And the place he was standing? Nothing grows there anymore. It's just a brown patch of dead grass, been that way for thirty years."

"How old is he?"

"I don't know. A little younger than my mom, so thirty-six or -seven. The whole thing is pretty weird. The guy who found him after he was hit died in a hunting accident a day later. The nurse had a miscarriage, and Dr. Garcia took up drinking and didn't stop until he died of cirrhosis of the liver three years ago."

"Yeah, right."

"It's true. They say when you shake his hand, sparks fly off the ends of his fingers."

"Are you saying that there aren't sparks that fly between us?"

"Sparks? No, not sparks. A whole forest fire." She gazed out the window for a moment, then turned back. "And no amount of rain can put it out."

Jewel studied her lover. Dante's shoulders were like a shoreline sloping gently downward. Her neck and arms were tan, but her belly and breasts were a shock of whiteness that seemed to glow, as if an inner lamp were burning. Jewel stroked her pale skin. The tang of salt on Dante's lips tasted like a whole ocean and the scent of her like special incense that sends smoke to the gods with wishes pinned to it. Her eye glinted like an opal. Jewel wanted to tell her lover these things, but the words were like a match trying to throw heat and light to the sun—they wouldn't even get close.

Dante climbed out of bed and leaned naked against the wall to stare out the window. The streetlight gleamed on the chrome of her bike and stretched its shadow down the street. The Diamond Cafe stood still and dark tonight, its picture window reversing the street and everything on it. Marlene must have fallen asleep, she thought. The hardware store was still, too, but a single bulb in back made a silhouette of the gardening tools, barbecues and cans of paint in the window. The small parking lot separating the store from the Empire was empty.

The stars were thin silver lights like nails not driven home. Where was the Milky Way? she wondered, stretching her neck to see every angle. The Chinese call it the Silver River, full of light and miracles and little class M stars glowing red like the lamp-flower from burning impure oil in an old-fashioned Chinese lamp. A falling lamp-flower was an omen promising the return of a lover. Dante imagined the wick tumbling to ash in front of her, then stared back at the street.

Darkness balanced on the lights of the street as if on the tips of bayonets. Dante felt her lover's hand slide up her back. When you meet a woman you see the parts of her body that she will use to please you. Her mouth and tongue and teeth and hands. You notice her fingers as she pushes back her hair, lifts a glass or writes a letter. You watch her lips as she whispers or laughs. You know she'll bring all this movement to your body—hands with long, tapering fingers, hands with broad strong palms, clumsy hands, graceful hands, strong, tender, rough, smooth. These hands will move on you with a certain sensitive heat and knowledge.

The town was close enough to the ocean for a salt chill to filter into the night air. Dante crossed her arms, suddenly aware that she was cold. She felt Jewel wrap her arms around her waist, a band of warmth.

Jewel looked over her lover's shoulder and out the window. The sky, she saw, was filled with needles of hope. She kissed Dante's neck. "Get back to bed. You'll freeze."

"I will." She leaned against Jewel.

Jewel slid her hands down the woman's back. "Nice ass."

"You're disgusting."

"I wouldn't be here if I wasn't." She kissed Dante's other shoulder and tugged at her hair. "Don't forget to put the toys away."

"I won't. Are you leaving now?"

"In a bit."

The air seemed even colder when Jewel's breasts were no longer pressed against Dante's shoulder blades, and she shivered. "Why were you so cruel to Donnie tonight, Jewel?"

"He asked my opinion, I gave it to him." Jewel sat on the bed and wrapped a blanket around her. "Do you have any cigarettes?"

"It wasn't very kind."

"His film was ugly. It was awful. The sooner he realizes that he's not an artist, the better."

"Who are you to say he's not an artist?"

"You thought it was terrible, too."

Dante said nothing.

"Now if you love me, light me a cigarette."

"You don't even see it, do you?"

"See what?" Jewel bounced off the bed to her feet, leaving the blanket. "The film was terrible. It was dumb. It was pointless."

"Why don't you get beyond the surface?"

"Scratch the surface and there's just more surface." Jewel grabbed her shirt off the floor. "What did you want me to do? I know Donnie Champlin. I've seen all sorts of his things and they're all the same—hopelessly bad."

"That's not for you to decide."

"He asked for my opinion. He asked. He wouldn't let me go till I told him. Synchronicity, Jesus Christ, as if long words make something worthwhile. And you played right along." Jewel yanked her shirt over her head, then searched the bureau for a cigarette. "God, what ugly furniture."

She found the pack and pulled out a cigarette. "Matches?"

Dante tossed her the book from the nightstand.

Jewel caught it with one hand. "Get into bed. Or put something on. You make me cold just looking at you."

She climbed back into bed, gathering the tangled sheets around her as Jewel lit a match, a single ugly flare in the room, then blew it out. Another lamp-flower, Dante thought suddenly.

Jewel dropped the matchbook and cigarettes onto the bureau. "Maybe I'm not as smart as you, but there are some things I do know. Like most Anglo men, Donnie believes if he works hard enough he'll get what he wants. Little Horatio Alger. But nothing's turning out for him, see? So he decided that he needs a woman to keep him going. A better half, someone who refuses to see that he fails because he has no talent. Guess who that someone is. Just guess who he wants to synchronize with."

"God, you are vain."

She blew out a stream of smoke. "Yes, I am vain. And I'm right. The saddest part is that the only woman who will stand up for him is Sue Potts, and he treats her worse than I treat him. Consider it divine retribution."

"There's no such thing and you don't give a shit for Sue Potts anyway."

"Of course I don't. If I wanted to make her miserable, I'd fuck the living daylights out of the man and leave him happy and crippled the rest of his life." She took the three steps over to the nightstand. One of Dante's eye patches was there, the strap folded neatly beneath the patch. She picked it up and examined the *C, F* and *B* embroidered in the velvet. The monogram was silver in this light, gleaming like the chrome on Dante's motorcycle or the light-fixture angels of the Empire. "What do these initials stand for?"

Dante sighed and held out her hand for the cigarette. "Why?"

Jewel handed it to her and watched as Dante inhaled. "Because I don't know your real name."

Dante returned it. "What difference does it make?"

"None."

"Then why ask?"

"Why not tell me?"

"Are you going to ask me about my eye next?" Dante touched her cheekbone below the empty eye socket.

"No." Jewel said, dropping the eye patch onto the nightstand, where the strap caught on the alarm clock. She pulled on her jeans. "Don't you believe in anything?"

"I believe in crossing the street to stay out of harm's way."

"How about god or art or any of that crap?"

"No, I don't think so."

"How about love?"

Dante burrowed into the covers. "No."

"Politics?"

Dante shook her head.

"Death?"

"Uh-uh."

"Anything?" Jewel said, exasperated.

"Gravity."

"Doesn't count. Gravity works no matter what you believe."

"That's true." Dante grinned. She looked away from her lover and out the window. She had the strangest feeling that she had somewhere, somehow gone through a mirror like Alice and had come back again. A moment ago she'd wanted Jewel to stay, spend the night, maybe move on with her when the time came, but now she felt Jewel wasn't leaving her fast enough. "So are you going to fuck Donnie?"

"God, no."

"Why not? He got herpes?"

"How about because I'm in love with you?" Jewel leaned over the bed to kiss her.

Dante pulled away. In the quiet night, the two looked at each other. Jewel's eyes were full and dark as if her pupils had expanded to their very edges to pull in every scrap of light.

Blowing a perfect smoke ring, Jewel stood up. "Why don't you just take me loving you for what it is?"

"What is it, Jewel?"

"A gift."

Dante paused. "Donnie's film was a gift."

"I know. And if I accept it, then I am obligated to him. That's how it is with gifts." Jewel stepped into her shoes.

Do you think I'm obligated to you, Jewel? Dante wanted to ask. "I don't think Donnie meant his gift that way."

"Right. Men never expect to get anything in return. Every offering comes with no strings attached." Jewel shook her head. "You'll never understand Donnie James Champlin, Dante. You'll never understand men."

"You're saying that you do? Fringe benefit from dancing naked for them at five bucks an hour plus tips?"

"And you think I'm cruel."

"I'm sorry."

Jewel dropped the cigarette on the floor and ground it out. "Go to hell."

There was a long pause. Dante listened to the rain. She didn't notice it beginning or ending anymore. It was a constant, like the equal sign in an equation. She didn't understand rain the way she understood fire, and she had the feeling that she didn't understand Jewel either. Trying to was like cutting water with a knife.

Finally Jewel spoke, her voice quiet. "You're going to leave me again, aren't you?"

"I never promised to stay."

"You're going and not taking me."

"You have things keeping you here."

"Like what? My house? It's sold. My job?" She gave a laugh that sounded like a stick breaking. "Pushing popcorn and smiling at creeps? At least in Tahoe I was behind glass where people couldn't touch me unless I wanted them to. I love you, Dante."

"I don't want you to. It's bad luck." Dante studied the silhouette of her lover. Bad luck? I've stopped carrying a rabbit's foot. Though it might have been good luck for me, it was definitely bad luck for the rabbit. Stopped picking up pennies to put in my shoes, first because it hurts to walk on them and second because somebody was bound to notice the extra jangling in my boots. If I was a guy in scruffy clothes with a bottle sticking out of my pocket, people would shrug and mutter, oh, he must be a vet. But since I'm a woman, they think I'm willing to do anything for cash—give head, fuck a dog, become a home video porn star.

Jewel broke into her reverie, her voice soft. "Tell me about luck. Tell me what it's like to have good luck. Tell me what I have to do to be lucky like you."

" 'What is this Luck, whose talons take in hand / All life's good things that go so pleasantly?' " Dante whispered, eye tightly closed. She opened her eye, and spoke to Jewel's outline. "Wish on the first star, just like Pinocchio. 'When you wish upon a star, makes no difference who you are.' "

Jewel smiled slowly at that. "Luck runs your life?"

"What do I know about luck? That's like asking a goldfish the meaning of water. You're born. You make noise. Then rigor mortis sets in. Believing in luck makes all that a little easier."

"Isn't lying bad luck?"

"Lying to whom?"

"To Donnie, for one."

"What harm could I do him?"

"What about lying to me?"

"I don't lie to you and it wouldn't matter if I did."

Jewel watched her for a moment. "Nothing touches you, does it? Not lying. Not love. Not even me."

She swung on her heel and was out of the room before Dante could answer. Is it true? Is she right? I let nothing touch me but gravity, as if I have a choice? Outside, the rain fell, the same rain that had fallen the night before and the night before that. It reminded her of an old gray aunt who comes in winter and stays all spring. Dante crossed her arms against the cold. Maybe I should've left yesterday. Why is it when I found her here, I felt like I'd been traveling forever just to feel this deep tingling thrill again?

While in Canada, she had found a candy-coated chewing gum called Thrills. Fourteen neatly packed pieces that she counted through the oval cellophane window. On the back was a drawing that looked like the purple-toothed smile from some Brothers Grimm monster, the teeth set edge to edge with little stars to show how shiny they are. The candy itself, a shock of lavender, cloves and soap, coated the roof of her mouth. It was delicate. Unusual. Addictive. And she had only five pieces left of the two boxes she'd bought at a small shop outside Toronto. How nice to have a box of thrills, she had thought, giving the clerk a handful of coins covered with pictures of animals.

The room was desolate in the feeble light. A raw, salty odor penetrated the old rug, the wood floor and the cracked walls. The familiar stink of bodies—sweat, hair and discomfort—oozed out of the corners of the room and transformed the walls into living things. She couldn't get used to it, even now that her own scent mixed with those of people who had come and gone.

These are the thin hours, when sadness grates against the windows and finally gets in. Walls between rooms and houses and time itself are less than half their daytime width. Shadows take on their own shapes, trees hunch and mutter, the air tingles with the courage to trespass. Faith is as fragile as a cobweb. Is faith that special kind of gravity? Why do I want so much to believe that? Why do

I want there to be something else pulling at me? If it wasn't for gravity—uncaring, unprejudiced, unthinking gravity—I'd be flung off the face of the earth and never missed. Is that why I want a special, specific kind of force meant for me? Why must such a question surface only at night, like a stray thought that's been reeled in? In these thin hours, even a lamp-flower would be welcome, or better yet, a hundred burning candles.

Dante pulled on the sweatshirt she slept in and stared out the window again. Like everyone else in town, in the daytime she could see the letters on the obelisk twenty feet up, the scarlet "GOD" gleaming as bold as sin. In the evening, when the neon letters spelling out the name of the theater glowed that it was show time, it took a practiced eye to find it. The scarlet disappeared in the red light. This late, with the sign turned off, she could only hope that the letters were still there and not faded away in the rain.

Virgil turned off the last light and locked the theater doors behind him. After sweeping the floors and polishing the glass doors, concession-stand counter and ticket-booth window, he had kneeled on the splintered floor near the screen and prayed. It would take more than one night to clear the Evil from the Empire. He had been lax. It wasn't only his small Evil that polluted the place. Pulling the hood of his parka over his head, he started walking slowly down the street. He liked to walk. It was like meditation and it calmed him. With the quiet sound of rain and the warmth of his jacket, he could walk for hours. The slam of a door made him lift his head to look up. Someone was crossing to his side of the street.

Jewel walked as quickly as she could from the boardinghouse and the streetlights. It was raining again. She hadn't noticed back in Dante's room. A woman has a tendency to forget such things in moments of passion and anger. Not that it mattered. For a second Jewel wished she could tear off the clothes she had just put on and let the cold rain seep into her pores. Maybe that would ease the anger and feed the sudden bewildering hunger she felt. It was a hunger to be home; she had to get home. Home had nothing to do with the house—a single-wide mobile home that looked like a square jersey cow hunched up on a bit of grass surrounded by a chain-link fence and a grasping line of hedge. Home was living with her mama, in spite of the ugliness at the end. Now Jewel had no home, only a place for a ghost to haunt. She had only a mirror and candles to fight against her loss.

Up ahead at the corner where she had to turn was the Sleep-Aire Mattress Company, closed for three years. Hector Martinez now used the parking lot to sell Christmas trees. Douglas fir, white pine, noble fir, Scotch pine, he had stenciled the names in red on a white board that leaned against the little hut with plastic sheeting for walls where he huddled with a thermos of coffee and a battery-powered space heater. The air smelled like oozing sap, the greenness of the scent always a surprise, though Jewel walked by here almost every day. She could see the trees leaning against one another like an exhausted forest. In a few weeks it would be thinned to almost nothing. Everyone in town bought their trees from Hector.

Why do young people leave their hometowns? Some say it's boredom, some say it's to escape their circumstances. Tonight, Jewel was sure that it was to escape the gods who live there. The god in the house who inhabits the mirrors when no one is looking. The god of pets who keeps them hidden when you get angry. The god of the kitchen who makes the oven heat up after you turn the switch. But Jewel hadn't left to escape her gods. She had made a pact with them and promised to return. She'd needed money, so she left town to become the favorite peep-show dancer at the Beaver Club in Lake Tahoe.

It had been a job. No different from stockbrokering, commodities trading, selling shoes or being a bank clerk, though there was a lot less money and a lot more grab-assing. Tahoe was beautiful, especially if you made an effort to get away from the tourists. The women she worked with were cynical and kind. They took care of one another. When Josie's little boy got the flu, Tanya, Alice and Jewel covered her shifts, even though it meant eight instead of the usual four hours of ultra-high heels. They celebrated birthdays and holidays and extra tips. They all hated the Beaver Club cheerfully and told stories of Mac the manager, an okay guy who didn't mess around on his wife, and Willie the owner, a greasy little jerk who did.

That had surprised Jewel more than anything. The only people who disgusted the topless-bottomless exotic dancers, the snake charmer with an act that caused the ASPCA to run riot, the touchie-feelie girls and the prostitutes were the married men who paid to see, touch, fuck or fantasize about them. Dirty jeans or a three-piece suit, Evangeline would say, cash is cash and spunk is spunk. Put a gold band on their fingers and they're all creeps.

Infidelity. What had bothered the women at the Beaver Club wasn't the sex or promiscuity, it was the broken vow. To Jewel the word *infidelity* had a high-tech ring to it, as if breaking promises were new. Perhaps the word had been invented when engineers first recorded static in stereo speakers, a tangled, high-pitched scrambling between songs. Maybe a broken promise caused the same kind of distortion in your brain, and it threaded down to your hands or feet or voice, making you say and do anything to blur out the promise you made to somebody not to do exactly what you were doing.

She realized that she had been walking on fallen leaves all the way home, each of them gold and crimson like five-fingered shoots of flame. On the trees, the few leaves left hung palms up as if begging the sun to come back. But there were hundreds plastered, flat and defeated, against the cold ground. They reminded her of soldiers who threw up their hands when they were shot, landing with their fingers splayed like starfish.

Dante watched the shadows as they swallowed up Jewel. Gone in the rain and the darkness. She moved away from the window and back to the bed. Maybe I should go now. Leave this soggy little town. Grabbing the rough wool blanket, Dante wrapped it around her shoulders. Slowly, she lifted her hand to her face and touched the delicate skin around her missing eye. While wearing a patch makes the empty place more sensitive to moving air or changes in temperature, it makes the rest of me invisible. Men don't hit on me, women won't talk to me, children stare. Wherever they look, all they see is what isn't there. Wherever I am, I am what is missing.

The rain popped in the gutters. Jewel liked the finger-snapping sound of it. Raindrops fell without a pinpoint of silence between them, and wet murmured through bare branches. At the corner stood a pine with its boughs heavy. Each drop on the tree held a single window of sparkling light, which, as she came closer, shifted and disappeared from one drop to appear in another. The light I see is different from the light someone ahead of me sees. The beauty I find is for me only, a kind of gold different from the reflection of light or the ring on a finger. A treasure. A promise.

The Firs Mobile Home Park had once had tall trees. Now there were only stumps. The roots had invaded the sewer system and the gas lines, but no one complained too loudly till the trees attacked the cable TV wires. The firs came down last spring, and now the only greenery left were the boughs painted on the broken sign, the lawn chairs with plastic weave in front of Albertini's and the ragged shrubbery that was only too happy to scrape any arm or leg that came near it.

Virgil followed her quietly. His boots made no sound as he walked down the wet sidewalk, and he stayed in the shadows so that if Jewel were to hear him, she wouldn't be able to see him. She must be cold, he thought as he studied her back. She's certainly getting wet. For a moment he wished he could be the rain falling on her. Splash her, seep into her hair and her clothes. I want to be for her like rain. He trotted down the other side of the mobile home, cutting through the Wedabakers' yard and ducking behind a shrub.

Jewel could remember the trees. What was left of them was split and stacked under Albertini's mobile home. Mama had liked Albertini—just about everyone did. He was a quiet man and a good neighbor. Behind his mobile home, he kept a rose trellis; in it stood a statue of the Virgin Mary with a head that fell off every winter. As soon as the daffodils bloomed, he would glue it back on. Every summer evening he would sit on the steps drinking one bottle of homemade beer for every two gin and tonics Mama drank. When she was nine, Jewel had gotten drunk for the very first time after she stole two bottles of his home brew.

Albertini was a lumberman who had retired before the lumber companies abandoned the hills and the valley. He was good with his hands and could carve, make wreaths, fix plumbing, lay sod, do all sorts of useful things even though he was missing the first two fingers of his left hand. He worked in a small room in his trailer that he called his studio, a neat place with tools and paint arranged on shelves, and sawdust and wood shavings swept into a pile and thrown into a barrel sitting in the corner. He would stay there from autumn till spring, coming out only to do odd jobs or to deliver a watercolor or a birdhouse with a tole design painted over the small door. Everybody in the county owned something by Albertini.

With the stroke he lost his words and the right side of his body. He got the language back sound by sound, but not his hand, and that defeated him. Jewel had watched him limp around his home, first with a cane, then a walker. His small garden became weed-infested, and the rosebushes grew so tall and thin that the heavy blooms hung almost to the ground. She hadn't seen Albertini for a while—he had asked her not to visit anymore, though she lived three spaces away—and she wondered if he used a wheelchair now and if he, like Mama, was having a hard time sleeping and hanging onto his skin.

Jewel knew Albertini was still alive; a county health nurse dropped by every other day to check on him. Jewel glanced over at his trailer; like the rest of the mobile homes, it was dark. She opened her door, flipped on the light and dropped her bag on the kitchen table. Shrugging out of her jacket, Jewel sat down at the table, the cigarette she had smoked now tasting sour.

Dante. From the first time I touched you, I loved you. The first time I touched you, I was invincible. I was the Joan of Arc of love carrying her shield around. For a moment, Jewel remembered Dante's slanting ribs with the structure of ferns, finding ropes of muscle and the tender skin on the inside of her arms, and the sweetness of Dante's breast filling her hand as if it were the whole world. Then you left and I saw my one chance at love riding away. Did you love me then? What made you stop? Where does love go once it's over? Is it beaten into nothing by rain? Does it slide from a body, speck by speck? Or get washed out? Does it dry in the sun and blow away? Does it turn into the dust that swirls in the sunshine when it's stirred up by a breath of wind? Does it burn away? Run? Melt like ice? Migrate like a flock of birds that gets lost on its way back, resigned to landing in a new place? Does it bicycle downhill, take a wrong turn, hit a grate and lie at the bottom, bruised and unconscious?

I swore I'd never do this again. I swore I would never let myself get burned again. Jewel squeezed her eyes shut. God, Mama, where are you when I need you? Where are you now? The last morning you could get out of bed by yourself, you stood there in your bedroom, hair matted and face too thin, looking shocked as if you just then understood your life was almost over. You stared right past me as if there on the nightstand between the *TV Guide* and your beads was a stack of lives like gloves waiting to be filled. And I saw, too, that I only had one chance in this life. After childhood, the machinery for hoping takes a while to get started up, but that morning I felt it. I could believe again. My life wouldn't be like yours, I was sure of it. But here I am, sitting in your chair, tasting the bitterness you tasted. Just how much distance is there between mothers and daughters?

It's so much easier to leave than be left. I sat on that ratty chair in the apartment in Tahoe after Dante disappeared, tears from wide-eyed crying warming my face. There was a single patch of sun on the rug that glided across the floor. I watched it till I had to leave for my shift at the club. The ache of it, her body being gone from mine, left me exposed to the elements. Now you, Mama. You've left me, too. Leaving me to be worn down by the rain. Don't tell me rain isn't strong. Drops can break huge boulders, shift the courses of rivers and ruin carnivals.

If there is a god of the Jews and the Christians, then I should be able to make a deal. Take my left hand, my right eye and both legs below the knee. I'll learn how to sit quiet and prim like an upright piano. I'll never wear anything but blue, gray or black, I'll save for my old age and I'll never cut my hair. Just bring her back. Bring Mama back.

Please let me get used to the feeling of not seeing her anymore. It's like getting used to very cold water, I know, stepping slowly in until you don't mind the numbness. If I don't learn how to look into my mother's face, the face she wore that night in the kitchen, then her whole self will be like a comet—here small and obscure, there brilliant and filling the sky, but either way moving too fast. The thought of her will come and go at its own interval.

Is life like that, a spot of brightness? Is love just supposed to fall on people like the blind sun on fields? There has to be a reason. There must be a plan, must be meaning in what happens—like Dante finding me—there's got to be. There she was, big as day, asking me for a ticket, a five-dollar bill in her hand, a smile on her face and her motorcycle parked out front. Mama was dead, my heart was mending and she shows up. Come to see a movie. Maybe it is luck, or some kind of curse. That special kind of gravity. Or synchronicity. But in spite of the ache and the joy and the doubt, for the last ten days she's made working at the Empire more than something that just happened to a person, like being manic-depressive or a debutante.

Mama kept whiskey in the cupboard above the refrigerator. Jewel glanced at the veneered wood. If I start drinking now, I won't want to stop. I'll stay in this house and get it delivered like Mama and turn into a recluse like Margaret Penhaligan.

Virgil slipped around to the front gate. The clasp had been broken for a long time. He'd once offered to fix it, but Jewel had said no, then gave him the strangest look. He realized what a mistake that had been. How could he know it was broken unless he'd been to her house? As far as she knew, he'd never even walked by. But he had been here a few times, often enough to know that her bedroom was in the back, her bedspread was pale blue, her vanity had a huge mirror cut in a half-circle and she liked to light candles and brush her hair before falling asleep. That was what Virgil liked the most—to watch her brush her hair. It was thick and fell just past her shoulders in a black wave. His hair was coarse and pale, like a pile of toothpicks. He hated it. Virgil crossed the lawn then crouched in the shadow of the mobile home and waited. The rain tapped against his jacket. Rain falls on the Just and Unjust alike, he thought absently.

Jewel could hear the soft rain fall against the tarred roof of the house, hushing everything. Rain, quiet and persistent like this, was almost friendly. Anonymous, soothing, consistent, no hammering beat demanding attention. Shutting her eyes, she sighed heavily and stretched, feeling her pulse in her muscles as she tensed. Clenching her jaw, she shut her eyes, concentrating on the beat. Why does my heart ache? Why ache and why my heart? People have used the heart as a symbol of love for hundreds of years. It is spattered on bathroom walls, bumper stickers and the arms of sailors. Nothing new about the heart.

But there is a moment, a single floating moment, when a woman and her lover melt into each other past skin and sweat, nerves and muscles. Hearts touch, the cells brush one another, they meet in the darkness, though bones and skin and logic will separate them in a moment. At this moment, similar to sunrise, when hope and possibility pour from the sky, these hearts touch and beat together.

And Dante betrays it. How can she do that? And why? Who can tell me? Oh, god, what does anybody know about traitors? Why is she here? What's going to happen to me? I hate money. I hate cars.

I hate telephones. I hate greed, I hate garbage and I hate banks. I do, however, like food. Jewel smiled and got up from the chair wearily. Funny how a few words can pyramid in the middle of the night.

Virgil sat still, the muscles in his legs beginning to tremble. He had spent four hours in prayer and now he didn't think he could keep on squatting in the grass like this. Maybe I should go home, he thought. More prayer is needed. If only I had a Sign to stay or to go. He counted to three under his breath, then placed his hand on the bib of his overalls. If she comes into the room now, I'll stay, he thought. Prove that the Evil of my dream last night has been destroyed. I can watch her, I can see her for what she is—a woman. A window to Death. I will triumph, oh Lord, I am worthy. If she lights a candle now, I will prove it to You.

The window remained dark. Virgil bowed his head, hand still over his heart. The Lord has another Test for me. He stood up slowly and walked away from the dark window.

I hate this town, Jewel thought suddenly, walking slowly back to her bedroom. I came back because Mama was dying. I pruned that awful hedge, I cleaned this house, I weeded the small garden. I gathered up the vegetables, cooked them and coaxed her to eat. There are still pumpkins and squash to harvest. When it got cold in the mornings, my breath a column of blue, the sun would glide over the frost and make it glitter like powdered diamonds, handfuls of diamond dust tossed onto the ground overnight.

Sitting at the vanity, Jewel lit the two candles, but the beautiful light did not calm her. My face looks harder tonight, she realized, taking the brush from her bag. She touched her tousled, damp hair. I love the way Dante caresses my hair, the way she cries out into it when she comes. Slowly, Jewel pulled her brush through the tangles. I carry the sound of her in my hair. It's the only thing she gives freely. What can I do? What will it take for Dante to not let me go? To take me with her? What will I have to do?

ten

•

SATURDAY NIGHT AT the theater was usually busier than the rest of the week. There wasn't much to do around town but drink, catch a flick or watch the apples fall out of the trees. Since it was autumn and the harvest was over, and since the state had raised the tax on alcohol, that left only the Empire with its double feature to distract those not wanting to spend too much money or one more night at home.

Jewel understood wanting to escape the four walls that seemed to shrink around a person because of the rain. The sky had cleared after a violent sunset, purplish clouds like bruises moving over the valley, and a brisk chill settled in the air. A night to get wrapped up in warm clothes, take a bottle from the stash you bought before the price went up and go sit on a back road looking at the stars. Jewel felt the urge to leave now. Find Dante, get on that bike. She glanced around the empty lobby. *Gaslight* had just started; soon the night's work would be over.

She couldn't run away tonight, but she'd be out of the mobile home tomorrow. She'd packed the last of the dishes, towels and other small things, and by the time she left for work, everything but her clothes was stacked into boxes. Alma promised to give all that stuff to Goodwill, Jewel thought, as long as I'm out tomorrow. Tapping the glass top of the concession stand, she poured herself some orange pop.

"Hey, darling," Dante called, her voice carrying across the lobby.

"Hey, yourself."

"I've been sitting in the dark so long, I'm starting to get stupid."

"You have plans for tonight?" Jewel smiled at her.

Dante didn't smile back.

"Are you all right? You're not angry about last night?"

"I'm not angry."

"So I'll see you later?"

"Sure," Dante answered, then walked away toward the women's bathroom.

Jewel watched Dante as she moved. Some say the world will end in fire, she thought, and I hope to god when I die, it's by the kind of fire she and I make. Burning bridges, burning fingers, burning the candle at both ends, just let me keep burning. I love it, I love watching it, I love making it. When gold is heated, impurities rise to the top, and touching her burns up all the boredom and doubt I gather.

The popcorn machine spluttered. What in the hell is wrong with it now? Jewel wondered. The power cable snapped, then crackled.

"Shit."

Back behind the stairs, Virgil stepped out of the janitor's closet. Not only did he store his cleaning stuff there, the circuit box was on the far wall. He closed the closet door and nodded to her.

"Virgil, were you messing with the electricity?"

He shook his head.

"Then what is wrong with this machine?"

Virgil shook his head again and twitched his shoulders. His hands were clasped inside the bib of his overalls, and for a minute she had a picture of him in her head, dressed like a Hollywood version of

Fu Manchu with the long silk sleeves of a kimono hiding a stiletto or a pistol. He walked over to the concession stand and peered over the glass counter at the machine.

"Maybe I ought to unplug it. Hit the circuit breaker."

"Can't. That would turn off the projectors upstairs."

"I can't unplug it till you turn off the circuit. It's one of those screw-in kind of plugs, you know?" Kneeling down, Jewel studied the power cable to the popcorn machine. What she didn't know about electricity could light up a medium-sized town. "We can turn the projector off for a second, don't you think?"

Virgil looked skeptical and shook his head for the third time.

He should wear a rattle on his forehead, so every time he does that you can just hear him shaking out a no, she thought dizzily. "This machine is a fucking hazard."

Virgil shrugged and pulled his hands out of his bib. They hung at his sides, huge and useless.

"So what am I supposed to do?"

"Wait," he answered, then hurried away.

Jewel heard a door squeak open and shut. He's gone down to the basement, goddamn it. Left me here with this tottering pile of electrical junk, just waiting to be turned to a crispy critter. Hell with it, then. I'm tired of being responsible. He doesn't care and he owns the place—do him some good to watch the Empire turned to cinders right in front of his eyes. Maybe I should call some-body—Bernie Tollett, or maybe Mendez. Like Bernie could do anything and Mendez even cares.

Looking up from where she was on the floor, she could see the smears, pits and scratches on the glass counter. Geez, if that isn't the perfect picture of a lifetime, she thought. Constantly getting leaned over, spilled on and scraped. Jewel also could see Dante's jacket folded neatly and placed on the shelf below hers. Reaching out, she touched the black leather covered with more scratches and pits. But Dante had earned hers facing the wind, while the Empire had received its through neglect. Jewel pulled the jacket off the shelf and unfolded it on her lap. It was heavy and double-stitched, and the collar had snaps on both sides so whether the zipper was open or closed, nothing would slap at the rider. Running her hands down the front of it, Jewel felt its strength, an easy durability that gave whoever was wearing it confidence that nothing from the outside could hurt her.

She ran her fingers across the zippered pockets that would cover Dante's breasts. The zippers were a dull silver, heavy-duty, with small silver beads that were tucked into the seams of the pockets. The buckles, two on each side with a length of leather between them, were chrome and still shiny. Dante had tightened the waist of the coat once and hadn't done it again. No epaulets. No studs, no sharp metal spikes protruding for show. No writing. This was a jacket for use, not a jacket for posing. Jewel loved the feel of it, liked to touch it when Dante wore it. She buried her face against the quilted lining. Dante's scent.

"Jewel?" a male voice called.

Shoving the jacket back on its shelf, Jewel scrambled to her feet. She managed to knock over her cup, and pop spread like flame over the cracked linoleum floor.

"Damn it!" she cried.

Donnie had finally steeled himself to come downstairs. When he saw Jewel jump up like a jack-in-the-box, he walked quickly to the concession stand. "I really got to talk to you."

"Not now, Donnie." She stretched over the mess to step from behind the counter and tossed a rag on the spill. Thank god the cup wasn't full, she thought, sighing. "You think we could turn off the movie for a second?"

"Why?"

"I have to unplug the popcorn machine, the cable gave off fireworks a minute ago."

"Seems okay now."

"What if it isn't?"

"Just be sure you unplug it as soon as we're done. It hasn't blown up yet, has it?"

"No, but—"

"Nothing's going to happen, and if it does, use the fire extinguisher. That's what it's for."

"Donnie—"

"Look, it's not important. None of this is important." Donnie grabbed her arm.

Jesus Christ, she thought. "What are you doing?"

He let go immediately. "Sorry. I just really got to talk to you and you're always doing something else."

"I'm busy, Donnie. I got to clean up this mess."

"How about tonight after the last reel? We could go for a drink or something."

Jewel sighed and glanced out the glass doors to the street. "I've got plans."

"How about tomorrow night?"

Why do people think persistence is a positive character trait? "No."

"So when?"

"Never. Now would you please just find Virgil for me?"

"I got to watch the projectors. I only came down for a second so we could talk."

"Then you just wasted your one second because I got nothing to say to you. Now either find Virgil or go back the booth."

"Why don't you want to talk?"

"Because I can't say what you want me to say, all right? Look, do you have an extra set of keys for this place?"

Donnie shrugged. "I thought you found your keys."

"Not for me, for Dante."

"She'll only need them if she stays in town," he said.

"It's getting too cold to ride a motorcycle."

"I don't know. She seems the determined type."

"You could say that." Jewel knew then, right then, with a sure knowledge that hit the base of her spine and shot up her back: My lover is leaving. Soon and for good. Dante, whose body is so beautiful and matches mine so well. I'll have a bed to myself again, my arms and legs untangled from hers completely.

"Jewel—"

She left Donnie standing near the counter and headed for the women's bathroom. I have to know, she decided. I need to know. I got a right to hear it from her.

Okay, that was stupid, Donnie thought. I shouldn't have grabbed her. He wanted to call out again, but couldn't think of anything that would make her stop, turn around and come back. "I can clean this up for you."

Jewel disappeared around the back of the staircase.

That was good, that was really superb. A real attention-getter. What am I going to do? Donnie sighed and stuffed his hands into his pockets. For a moment he felt like a character in an unintentional comedy, something along the lines of *Reefer Madness,* only his drug was a woman. That woman who just left him standing there. Slowly, as if his feet and legs belonged to someone else, he walked to the custodian closet and opened the door. Just get the mop, he thought to himself. Get the mop, get the bucket and go clean up her mess. She'll talk to you later. He reached for the light switch and froze. He could hear Jewel talking.

"Why do I feel so much when you feel nothing?"

"I told you how I feel."

Donnie memorized the path around everything he would have to dodge to get to the hole in the wall, then closed the door.

"You don't grab somebody's heart then twist her into loving you by shoving needles into it. Jesus, how cold you are."

"I don't act like that."

Dante, he thought, stepping up to the spot of light and looking through it.

"How would you know?" Grabbing Dante by her shirt front,

Jewel smashed a bruising kiss onto her mouth, then pulled back. "Don't pretend you don't feel this," she whispered fiercely, sinking her teeth into Dante's neck, her hands rushing for her clothing.

Dante pushed her away and turned to the door. With a single swift movement, Jewel had her against the wall, the yellowed tile cold against Dante's cheek and palms. Shoulder against her back, Jewel reached around and filled her hands with Dante's breasts.

"Don't move," she whispered, biting her ear.

"Let me go, Jewel," Dante whispered back.

Jewel found her nipples beneath the cotton shirt and rolled them between her fingers. Running her tongue from Dante's ear to her neck, she bit her again. Her own nipples hardened against Dante's back. Kneading, pulling, pinching, demanding with her left hand, she unbuttoned Dante's shirt with her right. Her hand reached under the cloth and she moved in closer, locking her lover against her. "Let me."

The tips of Dante's fingers found small ledges in the cracked tiles, and she gripped them as if for her life. Her head fell back against Jewel's shoulder, pushing her breasts further into her lover's hands.

Jewel kissed Dante's neck, taking small bites from one side to the other and back again. Dante's hips swayed against her as they rocked together. Like a dance, Jewel thought, biting again and hearing Dante's hiss of pleasure.

Goddamn. Donnie James almost swallowed his tongue. Jewel Mraz and Dante? At first, when he thought it was some kid's game as Jewel pushed Dante against the wall, he found the idea exciting that these two women would begin jerking each other off, or whatever it was women do. Till he saw Jewel's hand undoing Dante's faded jeans. Till he saw that hand sinking down, saw the grin on Jewel's face as if she'd found the treasure of the Sierra Madre when he knew damn well it was Dante's cunt she was playing with. He heard a low delighted laugh from Jewel as they rocked faster and faster.

Dante's fingers clenched then unclenched with the feeling, flattening her palms against the wall. She felt Jewel biting her neck, traveling down her shoulder and onto her back, sinking in her teeth. It hurt. It was exquisite. Jewel hung on with her teeth, fucking Dante as if she were giving all their future fucks at one time, there in the Empire Theater.

Donnie wished he wasn't seeing this. Donnie wished he was between them. Donnie lost his hard-on when he heard Dante's low moan matched by Jewel's. She's going to come, he thought. They're both going to come. In three seconds Dante was going to shatter into a million orgasmic pieces thanks to Jewel, and Donnie James Champlin would have given anything to be in her place. He twisted away from the bit of light, crashing into buckets and brooms to get out.

It wasn't a shattering. It was a welding. Dante could see the sparks behind her eyes when she came, the rocking, the heat, the juice that spilled from her and onto Jewel, all of these brought them closer together, binding them with pleasure and grace and fire.

From across the lobby, Virgil saw the door burst open and Donnie tear upstairs. What's that all about? There a rat in there or something? Serves him right if it bit him, he thought, shifting the toolbox to his left hand and crossing the lobby.

Where was Jewel? She'd spilled pop all over the floor. Probably looking for me in the basement, he thought. Just remember not to look at her, he instructed himself. Do not put your eyes on her. Eyes will lead you to Sin and she is Evil. Clean up the mess on the floor and prepare to Clean your Soul. He walked the frayed red-and-orange carpet to the broom closet.

"Liquid pearls," Jewel whispered, licking Dante's come off her hand.

Dante rolled her head on Jewel's shoulder, turning just enough to trade a crooked kiss. Though the room was spinning, the tile beneath her palms felt solid. So did Jewel's arm, which was still wrapped around her waist. I never knew she was so strong, Dante thought, realizing that Jewel had held her tightly the whole time.

"I don't want to turn around. I'm afraid if I look at you, you'll disappear."

"Now you know how I feel," she said softly into Dante's ear.

Virgil crossed the lobby and stepped into the closet. Peeking into the hole in the cinder block was an opportunity, one he believed had been given to him by God. He peeked. There was Jewel at the sink, washing her hands. She raised her head slowly and smiled at someone's reflection in the mirror. A beautiful smile. The kind of smile that could make a man fall in love, Virgil thought with a sudden pain. He couldn't take his eyes off her, till he realized that the person she was smiling at had just wrapped her arms around Jewel's waist and was kissing her neck.

Donnie sat on the stool in the projection booth. That explains everything. Why Jewel won't talk to me. Why she doesn't care about the painting anymore. Dante has turned her queer. She's got Jewel showing lust and passion that's mine. Mine, damn it. Clenching his jaw, he squeezed his eyes shut. His chest was aching so much he was gasping for breath.

Virgil stared through the hole into the ladies' restroom. His throat seemed to be caving in. It was Sin. No. More than Sin. Abomination.

"You're leaving, aren't you?"

Dante pulled away, lit a cigarette and blew a column of smoke at the mirror. "Yes."

"When?"

Virgil could smell the smoke. It's like the very stink of Lucifer, he thought, stumbling away from the wall. The Fallen Angel. The smell of the destruction of Sodom.

"I don't know." Dante turned away from the mirror to lean against the scarred door to one of the toilet stalls. The edge of the wood grain was a soft tan against the black paint. Why would anyone try to write on black? she thought. But already there was a muted rainbow of fingernail-polish graffiti on the walls. "Soon."

Donnie held his head in his hands. My god, my heart feels like it's getting crushed right out. He gulped down air, the smell of his sweat mixing with the stale air of the Empire.

When Jewel left, Dante was staring at a water stain on the ceiling. She lifted the cigarette to her lips and took a drag, feeling the heat of it through her fingers and her lips. Wonder if the Empire is too waterlogged to burn, she thought, following the outline of the stain with her eyes. Would it just smolder and leave a spot of grease and part of the stage curtain? Would it dry out and blaze, smoke coiling and the heat making the stars tremble and bend? Imagine the Empire on fire, flames joining hand to hand to dance around, twirling across the wood till there's nothing left.

Virgil was mopping the floor of the concession stand as Dante crossed the lobby, but he didn't raise his head to look. Lot's wife was turned to a pillar of salt by looking. I don't want that to happen to me.

Besides, you, Dante, should be glad I don't stare at you. The Wrath of God would fill my eyes and burn into your skin. It struck Virgil how Saul on the road to Damascus could become enraptured so easily through his vision. Beware even visions of angels, St. John Chrysostom said. Virgil knew that the eyes were the window of opportunity for Sin. The Righteous must look for the Signs, must prepare for the Judgment, must be cautious of the sights before their eyes so Evil could not plant itself in their Minds and souls with the pictures of Lust and Sin. He squeezed the gray-and-orange water from the mop and returned to cleaning the floor.

This ground must be cleansed. Sin has captured all of them but me, Abomination has followed and soon even I will no longer be protected. Give me a Sign. Give me direction, God. Fire is cleansing. Salt is cleansing, too, and there's a twenty-five-gallon bucket of it under the concession stand for the popcorn machine.

Donnie threw a preview reel as hard as he could against the wall. It crashed against the crumbling plaster and his film uncoiled onto the floor. Ought to take a torch to this place or a fucking nuclear warhead. Blow it to nothing. Less than nothing. Leave it a poison place where no one will ever get trapped again. He picked up a cup of pop from last night and whaled it across the room. Dammit. Most of it splashed onto the projectors.

He wished for death. No, not death exactly. Suicide, murder, unforeseen accident would crush his mother and father, who were entrenched in old ideas such as marriage lasting forever, getting ahead in life, art is found only in museums and children should outlive their parents. But he wanted to be nothing. To erase his existence, like Jimmy Stewart in *It's a Wonderful Life,* but with happier lives for everyone. That was how most people's lives were, anyway: Take them away from the scene and nobody would notice the void. You wouldn't realize that somehow the person who was meant to love you never managed to get born. As for Donnie, all that vanishing would require was the erasure of the haphazard daubs of paint, of the dreams and philosophies scrawled in wirebound notebooks. To not have been—not a memory, not a daydream, not a regret for anyone.

Grabbing his jacket, Donnie rushed from the room. He could go to the Mill, but do what? Sit with the others in silence. They sat in comfortable, relaxed positions, as if time passed easily for them. But you knew by their casual postures that they spent a great deal of effort dealing with the problem of time. How to speed it up, how to slow it down. The way they stood, moved, sat, drank, gave away how much time dragged like a shadow at their heels that blocked more than light.

All last summer Donnie had sweated for her. Nights became unsleepable. He had lain there conjuring Jewel—long legs he could feel wrapped around his waist and pulling him into her, her beautiful hands pressing on his back. He wanted to kiss those beautiful breasts, touch her mouth with his, caress the nape of her neck and rediscover the small, brown mole below her left ear. Instead of feeling the soft, tenacious grip of being inside her, he made love to the darkness instead.

And now he would never touch her. Ever. He was almost

running in the darkness toward home. The lights in the house were off, as they usually were, though his mother had turned on the light above the stairs to his garage apartment. He took the steps two at a time, reaching the top feeling winded and slightly dizzy. It wasn't from exertion but from gasping for air and the pain in his chest. For a moment he thought it was a heart attack, and as he opened the door, he realized he was right. A heart attack—not the kind that had to do with hospitals and nitroglycerin pills, but the kind in tragedies and Hollywood musicals. His heart wasn't crushed out, but breaking to bits in his chest.

Donnie didn't bother turning on the lights. He grabbed the canvas from the easel and flung it from the top of the stairs into the backyard. From the garage he took the box of wooden matches and the charcoal lighter his father always left on a shelf in the garage. Dropping the painting on the grass, he poured the fluid onto the image of Jewel. With his thumbnail, he lit a match, the head spluttering to life, and threw it on the painting.

The liquid fire caressed the canvas. Jewel seemed to be shifting inside the fire, flickering like flame itself as he watched it burn. It's over now, he thought, still struggling to regain his breath. His heart still hurt. The fire began biting at the fabric. The paint was giving off an acrid, sour smell that tasted like tar. Dashing back upstairs, he returned just as Jewel's unfinished face was disappearing to ash. In his arms were paintings and sketches. He dropped them, then began building a pyramid over the fire with the canvas frames. Smoke puffed between the paintings as he laid them against one another. A stack of onionskin sketches caught quickly, brilliant sheets of gold.

From his back pocket came the sketchpad filled with Jewel that he always carried. He had spent the summer sketching her. At home, at work, each line brought her beauty closer; he placed the details of her before him one by one, then pulled back to savor them. In the kitchen one summer night, staring at the dark windows across the yards of the neighbors, he realized that with every scrap of paper he had fallen more deeply in love with her. He looked at the sketches now. Covered with delicate lines and shading formed by his blunt fingers smearing the pencil, the paper became tattered and thin in his hands, while the pad had permanently curved to fit him.

Donnie pushed it into the fire, the pages flying open and leaving themselves more vulnerable to flame. Destroy it all. Let fire burn out my ambition and my dreams as it burns away my attempts to make something permanent in this life.

eleven

•

DANTE STOOD INSIDE the projection booth. She had picked up the small reel from off the floor and wound up the film, then glanced at the huge film reels spinning on the projector. A wheel, indefatigable symbol of technology. These wheels, they aren't the sunwheel, or the Great Wheel, or Ezekiel's wheel in the air. They're wheels like car tires and gears, designed to capture and hold pictures once they've passed the light of the projector. MacLeish said that a world ends when its metaphor has died. It perishes when those images, though seen, no longer mean anything. Dante blinked and stared at the white light of the projector hitting the film. She could almost see the heat warping the air and she thought, Prometheus, Mithra and Raven have faded, as their gifts became as common as a matchbook.

She set the film can on the counter. Don't think about it, she decided. Philosophy is great as long as you can sit under a tree and don't need to worry about love or everyday living. With a rag, she wiped up the pop off the floor and the projectors, and threw the rag and the empty cup into the garbage can. Where is Donnie and what the hell am I supposed to do with this movie projector? Geez.

She studied the reels as they spun. We have a little bit of time, maybe Jewel knows how to run this thing. Dante looked at the knobs and buttons. Looks pretty complicated. I'll just turn it off when the movie's over.

Dante sighed. She glanced again at the bright light behind the film that made the chrome gleam. A small victory: For once no such band of gold lit up her mind, making her think of faraway places and ideas. Her thoughts remained in the Empire, leaving her to feel cloudy and chilled like the valley itself, as if she'd finally forgotten everything that had given her substance and shadow. Even when it wasn't raining here, it seemed to be raining. Even when it wasn't cold, it felt cold. Even when you were alone, you weren't alone. The valley itself was haunted by ghosts just as sure as Dante was haunted by her own.

I was wrong. There are more ghosts here than in the desert. A ghost for every drop of rain, they haunt this small town because there's no way out. Believing in heaven, believing in the good life, believing in anything will not lift you over the mountains and over the county line, will not bring peace. There is only here and it catches at a person like the blackberry brambles.

What a strange idea. Ghosts and hauntings. My own restlessness has got me thinking out beyond the edge. She knew letting her mind wander meant unhooking strange ideas like little bats that flapped around, letting out little shrieks. What is this love? She felt like a traveler who for years has read about poltergeists but never expected to be face to face with one. Why does my heart ache? What am I doing and what am I going to do? So now I've found love and I know I want to run away from it.

To take off all your clothes and lie down next to someone is extremely risky. The odds are it won't work out—you could be laughed at or hurt. Your lover could be selfish or clumsy or incompetent. The risks are so high, it's a wonder anyone would take such a chance. Usually in such a situation, though, you aren't in your right mind. You couldn't be in your right mind. But to fall in love?

You have to return to your right mind and fall in love while breaking all the slowly built habits of self-preservation.

Jewel looked up as Dante came bounding down the stairs. She smiled softly, but Dante didn't smile back.

"We've got a small problem," she said when she reached the concession stand. "Donnie's gone. We'll have to deal with the projector."

Jewel sighed. "Great. First that fucking popcorn machine and now this."

"What's the matter with the popcorn machine?"

"Nothing that doesn't mean electrocution. Remind me to unplug it before we leave."

As if on cue, there was another snap and a sharp pop from the power cord.

"Jewel!" Dante cried.

Sparks shot out across the worn linoleum, several landing on the bare wood floor as the cable twisted like a snake. Jumping sideways, the power cord split in half. Jewel tore away from the counter, heading for the janitor's closet. Forget the movie, she decided, pulling open the door and turning on the light. She stepped up to the circuit box. With both hands, she pushed the master switch and the Empire went dark and quiet.

The cable stopped hissing. On hands and knees, Dante scrambled across the floor. She pulled her leather jacket from the shelf and took a book of matches from the pocket. The small flame was plenty to find her way to the wall socket. A single screw held in the plug. Damn, she thought. Where can I find a screwdriver? Wrapping the cable around her fist, she braced her feet against the wall and pulled. Success. The screw was stripped and the plug came out easily.

"Okay," Dante called to Jewel. "Turn the lights back on!"

Jewel switched the master breaker back. She leaned against the wall, looking at the ceiling. The closet smelled like pop and dirty water, a sickening smell. After cleaning up the concession-stand floor, Virgil had left the bucket inside the door without emptying it. The mop hadn't been rinsed out either. Strange. He's never done that before, she thought. Staring straight ahead, she noticed in the crumbling cinder block a small hole. Stepping over to the door, she turned out the light and looked back. The hole was almost glowing. Not much, but enough if you knew where to look.

Jewel wondered later why she'd been surprised when she looked through it. Of course Donnie or Virgil, or both of them, would have something like this. Juvenile kicks, what else could you expect?

"You're not going to believe what I found," she said, returning to the concession stand and Dante.

Dante stuffed the matches back and tossed her leather jacket on the counter. "What?"

"A hole in the closet wall that looks into the women's can."

Dante didn't say anything. She wasn't even looking at Jewel. "What's that smell?"

"I don't smell anything."

Dante stepped over to the dead popcorn machine and looked at the floor. "You don't smell that? Smells like something's burning."

"Something was burning—the cord."

"No," Dante shook her head. "That's not it."

Jewel stepped behind the counter. "Hand me that fire extinguisher, would you?"

Dante swung it over. Jewel pulled the pin, aimed the nozzle and squeezed the lever. Nothing happened. She tried again. Nothing.

"Great. Good thing we weren't relying on that before."

With a sharp movement, Jewel threw the extinguisher across the lobby. It smashed into the wall next to the door, leaving an imprint. The glass counter on which Jewel slammed both fists did not crack, though Dante was sure it would.

"I can't fucking believe it. Doesn't fucking work. This place could've gone up in flames and here we'd be, getting toasted trying to put it out."

"Take it easy, Jewel."

"No! Goddamn it, no! What are they thinking?"

"Why are you even surprised?"

Jewel paused for a moment. Good question, she thought.

"Why do you expect things to work the way people say they will?"

The heavy wooden door between the lobby and the theater swung open.

"What the hell happened to the movie?" a man asked, both his hands palm up.

"I'll go take a look," Dante muttered.

Jewel nodded. "Looks like we're having technical difficulties."

"Uh-huh," he said, nodding.

Others wandered over to the concession stand. Jewel looked at them and sighed. "Look, why doesn't everybody call it a night, okay? Why don't I give everybody some free tickets and you can come back whenever you want?"

"What about a refund, too?" the man asked.

"I can't give you a refund now. I've already gone to the bank," she lied, smiling. He smiled back. Got him, she thought. "Come back tomorrow, okay? Bring your ticket stub."

Dante stepped into the projection booth. The last reel of *Gaslight* was all over the floor, looking like a pencil drawing by a schizophrenic. Great, she thought. The projector was still on, throwing a blast of light against the screen. Stepping around the loops of film spilling all over the floor, she stepped to the power box and turned off the projector. The machine went dark and quiet, just as the houselights came up.

Tonight. I'm leaving tonight. She knew it as sure as she knew that darkness would come when she shut off the light.

twelve

•

JEWEL ARCHED AGAIN. Dante loosened her hold, then dragged her fingers across Jewel's soft belly, sliding over the ridge of her hip bone and down her leg. Against her mouth, she could feel Jewel's pulse pounding, the blood rushing beneath her clit. Dante pulled away gently, dragging her tongue along Jewel's back.

Dante sat up, her hands tracing Jewel's curves. By the reflected light of the street lamp, Dante could see Jewel's eyes were shut as she took great gasps of air. They were both sweating; the window was fogged by their heat and sweat stung the scratches along Dante's back and ass as she moved. Catlike, with a quick grace, she lay down again and kissed her lover's mouth.

"You taste like me," Jewel whispered, not opening her eyes.

Dante kissed her neck, leaving a trail of bites along the muscle behind her ear down to her collarbone. Like a dance, she swept Jewel's skin, following the touch of her fingers with that of her mouth. She kissed her again, drinking in her whole mouth, then kissed the triangular birthmark, nibbled on her nipples, licked the half moon under her breasts to catch a single drop of sweat curving around to her back. On Jewel's shoulder blade was a bite mark, distinct even in the hazy light and a twin to the one on her neck. Dante smiled softly, kissing the purple bruise, brushing her skin.

Later, as she lay still with her head resting on Jewel's breast, she studied the flower-print drape. In the day, the colors were a dullish orange and red, the flowers the size of dinner plates. Nothing had ever grown like that in nature, she was sure. At night, though, the pictures seemed to have a different meaning. Right along the opening where the curtains joined, there were two flowers that mismatched each other. Two half-circles that fell together. From this angle, Dante thought it looked like a crude drawing of a human brain, there on her curtains.

She knew what a brain looked like. In third grade, the teacher had brought in a plastic model—gray, canyoned and greasy to touch—to Dante's classroom. It came apart to show the different parts. Hippocampus, cerebrum, cerebellum. The names, which she had to memorize for a science test on which she got a B, never quite fit. They sounded more like musical terms—adagio, andante, allegro, medulla oblongata. Tonight, she could remember it so clearly. She could even remember wondering which parts were the smart parts, which were dumb. Which were for love and for hate and for thinking up games. Which part understood money and which part was in charge of colors. There were no musical names for those. There were no sections with color-coded index cards to explain where they were.

Now she wondered again. What part of the mind remembers? What part of the mind rejects? Why is love connected to the heart and why is strength connected to the hands? What part of me is made fast to Jewel, bound as sure as light is to fire, and what part of her is tied to me?

Dante sat up and reached for the cigarettes. "Do you want one?"

"No thanks."

Dante pulled one out of the pack and lit it. She sat on the edge of the bed, surveying her belongings. Not much to gather up, she decided, rubbing her face with her hand.

"Are you leaving tonight?" Jewel asked quietly from the bed.

"In the morning." Dante pulled in a lungful of smoke.

"Are you taking me with you?"

Dante crossed her arms and watched the wisps of smoke slip from dark to light in the bedroom. "I don't know."

Jewel sat up. "You're not."

"I never said I would."

Jewel threw the blankets in a heap when she got up. "Why do you abandon me?"

"I don't abandon you."

"What do you call it?"

"I never said I would stay, Jewel."

"Yes, you did. You promised to stay with me, here or on the road."

"When?"

"Right now. Last night. The night before. Every time you touch me you make that promise," Jewel said urgently. She knelt on the floor and looked up at her lover's face. Don't turn away from me, Dante.

Dante shook her head and did not look at her. "That's not true."

"Not true to who?"

"I never made any promises, Jewel." She took a drag from her cigarette.

"Your hands did." Jewel laid her right hand between Dante's breasts, then slid it up to her face. "Your lips, your body—every time you touch me you bind me to you. Why would I let you go? Why would you leave me behind?"

Dante turned her gaze toward her. She is the most beautiful woman I have ever seen. "This is where you belong."

"Wherever I am is where I belong."

Dante slid her hand through her lover's long hair, a habit she had instantly regretted acquiring. She took a deep pull from the cigarette and let out the smoke. "Some people need a place. They grow into it and nothing can cut them free. Some people rely on a place to keep them on their feet."

"You don't need a place?"

"No. But you do."

"You owe me, Dante."

Do I owe her? Did I promise? Am I obligated to pay? Dante dropped the burning cigarette into a small ashtray on the night-stand. She studied the young woman kneeling on the floor. She's a stranger again, Dante realized. Beautiful, but still a stranger, and she has grabbed hold of me like a shield. I want you, Jewel Mraz. I want you to fall back on my bed with your hair feathering the pillow this last night. "I do love you, Jewel."

"But you're leaving me."

"Love's not enough. This small town has a powerful field of gravity and leaving it would be like playing Red Rover. You run as fast as you can, keeping your chin down. Aim for the weakest link, the loosest pair of hands, and smash through to freedom." Dante leaned over and hugged Jewel to her. "Love doesn't have the right kind of momentum."

Jewel's chin was on Dante's shoulder. She could see their shadows on the opposite wall, two uneven shapes. "Who says?"

"Love is a staying-still thing."

"You're wrong."

"If you love someone, you will stand still, let your feet become part of the earth. You stop moving."

Jewel pulled away. She suddenly realized how cold the air was and shivered. "Not if you move together."

"What, you think we'll start vibrating at the same time? Pick up each other's walk? Come six times a night at exactly the same second?"

"You know that's not what I mean."

"What do you mean, Jewel? What are you saying to me?"

"We are supposed to be together. This is meant to be." She crossed her arms and tried to rub warmth into her skin.

"Fate? You, talking about fate? What you're talking about are a couple of coincidences and your determination to make them mean something."

"I love you."

"That's not my fault." Dante tugged a blanket out of the heap of bedclothes and handed it to Jewel. "You look cold."

Jewel ignored it. "Don't leave me behind. Don't treat this as nothing. Don't let this become nothing."

"My god." Dante's arm, with the blanket, dropped back on the bed. "You know what you remind me of? One of those TV preachers telling people that if you're Jesus-fearing, you'll get ahead in life, win prizes, succeed in business, anything you want. And if you're not getting ahead, you're a godforsaken piece of trash destined for death and the gutter. But it's not Jesus you're misrepresenting. It's love."

The way Dante stretched out the word love to twice its length made Jewel clench her jaw. Studying her lover, she realized that they were like two people leaning forward to throw stones at each other from separate mountain peaks, unaware of the dangerous drop between them. *She'll let me go,* Jewel knew. *She's letting this go. And what was I thinking? That I could convince her to stay? That love was all the glue she needed to stay with me? That we'd ride off into the sunset? Damn, I've been watching too many movies. Thinking I could break away from this small town, fall in love with the woman of my dreams. All I need is the winning lottery ticket and I am set. I have almost the same odds of winning as I have of making this love work.*

117

thirteen

•

DANTE BEGAN PULLING on her clothes as soon as the bedroom door closed behind Jewel. It would only take minutes to throw her clothes into the saddlebags, pull on the helmet, get that bike started and tear out of town. Go. Leave. Get away. She pulled on her boots, then glanced out the window. Jewel was walking down the block. Will I ever see her again? Dante wondered. Probably not. Will I want to? Probably. Will I want her? Yes. Dante slid on an eye patch.

It had amazed her, the first time she and Jewel had made love, that Jewel took off the patch. Everybody secretly wanted to know what was underneath it, but Dante had learned that nobody really wanted to look. That first time, Jewel had reached up to her face with both hands and slid the patch away. It was so easy for her to do, just another article of clothing getting in the way of having her lover naked. This had never happened to Dante, to find someone so sure of herself that she accepted all of Dante as she was.

Dante was nine years old when the accident happened. The doctors had said something about sympathetic nerves in the eyes, how the failure of one will cause a failure in the other, so both were bandaged closed. She lay back in the bed, surrounded by a confusion of noise she had never noticed. The soft rush of air from a vent, the rattling of the windowpane as the wind hit it. Slices of what had started out as words echoing down the hall and around the corner of her door. The way footsteps changed pitch as they drew near, passed and walked on. Scraps of music, TV shows and squeaks from the hard rubber wheels of stretchers, wheelchairs and electronic equipment.

The smells were jumbled, too. Disinfectant became comforting; so did the Ivory soap and Keri Lotion of the nurses. Bridge-party perfume and cigarettes meant her mother was near. Car exhaust, Aqua Velva and another smell that reminded her of unsweetened cocoa was her father, usually rustling the bow on a stuffed animal. Her older brother, Robbie, smelled like rain and sounded like jingling coins as he walked.

Late at night when it was quiet and the sound of the air from the vent seemed to hush even the few sounds left, she would smell flowers, as if every bouquet that had come into the room had rubbed its scent into the walls to ooze out at night. They wrapped around her, scents too sweet and too full to be comforting. She would lie still as long as she could, then pull the sheet over her head. Only halfway; she didn't want the night nurse to think she had died.

She never told her father that Robbie, while shooting pop cans with Todd Nielsen's Daisy Rough Rider, had taken a potshot at a livelier target. And she never blamed him. Even at the age of nine Dante knew that if there was no risk, there was no fun.

She turned away from the window. Tucking her clock and other eye patches in a saddlebag, she pulled on her jacket. It suddenly occurred to her that in the twenty years following the accident, she had learned that there were more dangers than the physical ones. Dante stopped packing the saddlebag and peered over her shoulder through the window again. Jewel had just faded into a shadow. If I run, Dante thought, I could catch her. She stood still, staring at the darkness into which her lover had disappeared. Dante blinked. Turning, she faced the other window, the one with the flowered curtain. The picture didn't look like a brain anymore, only two ugly mismatched designs. Outside the glass was only a small town that meant nothing to her, a town that would be the same after she left as it had been when she arrived. She glanced again at the window that had framed Jewel as she walked away. Only now a man with the hood of his jacket up moved steadily down the sidewalk.

Dante left the side of the bed and stepped to the window. Who the hell is that? she wondered. She leaned on the sill, the dust on the ledge smelling acrid. His walk is familiar. So is the jacket. Virgil Penhaligan. Going the wrong direction, she knew. Even newcomers know where the Penhaligan house is. He's following Jewel, she realized, spinning from the window.

fourteen

•

DONNIE HEARD THE door open. A light went on. Jewel was home. Go out or wait? He looked around her small bedroom. He could see himself now in the half-circle mirror of her vanity, sitting on the bed. His hair was wild. What am I doing? he thought suddenly. He had slipped in the front door, which she always kept unlocked, and crept through the mobile home to her room. Sitting there in the darkness, he had had a creepy feeling. A woman died here not too long ago. Maybe there are such things as ghosts, maybe Jewel's mother will come down the hallway after me, ready to protect her little baby.

But since Jewel wasn't home, there was nothing for a ghost to protect. And I'm not a threat, he had wanted to call. I love her. I would never hurt her, I just want to talk to her. He blinked his eyes, ran his fingers through his hair and took a deep breath to slow down his heart. It was pounding so hard that for a moment he thought it would spring out of his chest. Another one of those heart attacks of a different sort. His neck was tight. The muscles in his back became pins that cornered his nerves and stabbed at them. Let her understand, let her hear me, let her ask me to stay.

Virgil squinted. The curtains around Jewel's window were gone. Leaning forward and craning his neck, Virgil suddenly saw a man sitting on the edge of her bed, hunched over his knees. What it looks like, he thought, is that statue, *The Thinker*.

Dante couldn't see into the mobile home, but she had a very good idea whose window Virgil was trying to look into. She had followed every step, realizing, when he ducked through the hedge without a sound, that he had obviously followed Jewel home before. Dante had gotten caught in the straggling shrubs. Thank god for leather, she'd thought, pulling free. She was relieved that Virgil hadn't heard her, and now she stood ten feet away, glancing from the dark window to him.

Slipping out his right arm, then his left, Donnie took off his jacket. Searching for a place to put it, he realized her room was almost bare. Nothing on the walls, the closet empty, the top of the vanity naked but for a hairbrush, a book of matches and two tall candles. Boxes. She had stacked boxes along the wall. Next to the door was a small suitcase with the sleeve of a shirt hanging out. She's leaving, Donnie realized. She's leaving town again. No, god, no. He heard his breath rasp, trapped like a bird in his chest. No, it can't, won't happen.

The hall light went on and the man lifted his head. Donnie James Champlin. The recognition struck Virgil like a punch to the heart, the pain spreading like fire in dry grass, licking its way along.

Donnie's heart squeezed as if his blood had suddenly become too heavy to be pumped. He was dizzy again, his temples feeling stretched by the effort of his heart. Just breathe and keep on breathing, he thought, dropping his jacket on the bed. Jewel was coming into the bedroom.

Jewel swung open the half-closed door and flipped on the light switch with a practiced swing of her arm.

"Jesus Christ!" she shouted, stepping back from the crouched man on her bed.

"Jewel!" He leapt to his feet.

"Donnie! Shit! No, don't move! Stay where you fucking are."
She leaned against the wall outside of the room.

Virgil heard the sound of her voice through the glass and the
rain. She was standing back, her eyes wide and mouth open. He
waited. What could he do? Help her. I'll help her, he decided, still
watching as Donnie stepped toward her, arms outstretched.

The sudden light made Virgil's face glow like a Renaissance
painting of a saint, with his shaggy hair and beard, and his eyes
peering up as if to god. Dante watched him kneeling in the light,
then suddenly realized that if Virgil were to look in her direction,
he would spot her easily. Stepping back, she almost slipped on the
damp grass. Careful, Dante thought, tucking her chin into her
jacket, sure the overgrown bushes would hide her completely.

"I'm sorry, I'm sorry," Donnie repeated over and over. "Jewel,
please, I didn't mean to scare you. Can I get you something, a glass
of water, anything?"

She rubbed her forehead with her hand. Just as I was getting
sleepy, now my nerves have been stretched and snapped awake.
She held her hand up. "Don't touch me. I'm fine. Just sit down.
Sit down."

He sat back on the bed.

Pushing against the wall, she stood up and walked through the
door. "Let me catch my breath so I can tell you to get the hell out
of my house."

"I'm sorry, I just, I had to talk to you."

Jewel leaned against the door frame. He looks awful, she noticed.
So pale, the blue shadow of his beard seems to take over his face,
and the way he's dressed is almost disgraceful. "Your shirt's inside
out."

The light from Jewel's bedroom sprinkled the grass with beads
of gold. Virgil glanced from them to the two people in the house.
Donnie James Champlin slowly pulled his shirt over his head, the
outlines of his body hazy in the weak light. Virgil's eyes opened
wider. That's it. That's the rest of the Evil I have been feeling.

Donnie James Champlin and Jewel. Dante and Jewel. Jewel is the Fallen Woman, a Gate to Hell, Impure, horrible, a Demon and Certain Death. She is Sin. Sin. He scurried backward as if what he was seeing was burning his eyes. He turned to run, his boots squeaking on the lawn, part of a shrub clawing across his face.

"What was that?" Jewel said, craning her neck to peer out the window. She saw her reflection in the glass, her outline weak. Donnie's back was a blurred rectangle of color.

Dante watched Virgil disappear into the shadows, then stuffed her hands into her pockets. She was cold, she wanted a cigarette and some sleep, but something was keeping her here. Dante looked around for any sign of waking neighbors, then stepped carefully back in the shrubs to take the place Virgil had occupied. From here she could see perfectly into Jewel's room. Jewel herself was looking out the window. She is lovely, Dante thought. Then she saw Donnie, struggling with his shirt. What the hell is this?

Donnie yanked his shirt back on, right way around and the right way out. "What?"

"I thought I saw something," Jewel murmured, still studying her reflection in the window. My hair and eyes are so black, like the night itself is resting in them. My skin is golden, so unlike Dante's. She has a constellation of freckles on the soft spot of her belly, a little cluster like the Seven Sisters below her breastbone. I touch her and kiss her, but there are times when it seems a thin sheet of glass is between us and all I can touch is the perfect, smooth shell of her.

"Is this better?" Donnie asked, plucking at the front of his shirt.

Jewel sighed and looked at him. No way to get out of this, she decided. "Yeah."

"Look," Donnie began, staring at the floor. "I'm really sorry about scaring you, I didn't mean to. I guess I wasn't thinking, but I just got to tell you some things."

"Can't we talk about this later, like after the sun comes up?"

"I got to tell you—"

"Why did you leave work early?"

"I—" He looked up. "I saw the two of you."

"Saw us?"

"In the Empire."

Jewel understood immediately. "Through the hole in the wall."

"Yes. I saw you with Dante. I saw you—"

"You saw us fucking," she said bluntly.

"Yeah," he whispered. "I left. I couldn't stay."

Jewel squeezed her eyes shut. *Half an hour ago I was with Dante and we were trying on each other's skin. I wish, I wish, I wish I had stayed there. Stayed in that narrow bed with her. Broken the glass between us. Perhaps she would be staying here if I did. Maybe she would be taking me when she goes. And maybe she's right— love is a standing-still thing and she's like fire, always needing to move.* "Go home, Donnie."

Dante put her hand on the ground, then pulled it back. The ground felt damp, cold and barely strong enough to hold them all. *Donnie James and Jewel? Did his dream come true? Will it come true now that I'm leaving? Would Jewel accept him in my place? Maybe they could have a chance Jewel and I will never have.*

Donnie held up his hand, then let it drop. "You could be a little nicer about this, Jewel."

"You broke into my house, remember? Don't even try to tell me to be nice."

"But when a man is trying to admit he made a mistake and is trying to explain—"

"—he better not expect a lot of tolerance at four o'clock in the morning." She turned to the vanity and picked up the book of matches.

"Please. I wanted to paint you. Wanted to immortalize you in oil."

"Great. I'll file that along with 'I'll put you in my memoirs,' 'I'll write you a song,' and 'Baby, I'm going to make you a star.'"

"Jewel."

"What do you want me to say?" she asked, not taking her eyes

125

from the matchbook balanced in her fingers. "What? Why don't you take out a piece of paper and a pencil and write down exactly what you want to hear. I'll pretend I'm a forty-dollar hooker and try to say it like I mean it."

Glancing at the mirror, she saw he was wincing. A shock of pity hit her. "Say what you got to say. I'm listening."

"I was trying to get you to fall in love with me. I thought that . . . but then I saw you, with Dante. I saw what I didn't have. What I'll never have."

What I'll never have, she thought, looking at her reflection in the mirror and crushing the matches in her fist.

Dante couldn't hear what they were saying, but she recognized the expression on her lover's face: bleak hopelessness, a sadness not charged with anger. Jewel stood with her back to Donnie, her fist clenched in front of her own face.

Donnie's body felt like its reflection in water. He was shaking. "All of the paintings. The sketches. Every last thing, gone in the fire."

"Fire?"

"I burned them. Gone, gone, gone . . ." His voice faded away. He felt his heart beating against his skin so hard he could barely catch his breath. Suddenly the room seemed smaller; the boxes multiplied within his sight. "You're leaving town, aren't you?"

"Yes."

"With her?"

"No," she whispered.

"Where are you going?"

"I don't know."

Donnie stood up and stepped toward her. "Then stay."

"With you?"

"Or without me." His face grew larger in the mirror, and she could see the edges of his teeth were scalloped like seashells.

"No."

"Are you going back to Lake Tahoe?"

Stepping around him, she leaned against the door frame. The matchbook cover lay slick and hot in her palm. "Maybe. At least I'd have work."

With a burst of strength, Donnie lifted one of the moving boxes stacked against the wall and hurled it at the vanity. The candles flattened, bouncing away, and the mirror crashed, shards falling to the floor like daggers.

Dante stood up. What to do now? She wanted to rush around the side of the trailer to the front door, but froze instead. What am I going to do, gallop in like the cavalry? Turning to the left, then spinning to the right, she saw the mobile-home park was still dark and quiet. No one else had heard the sound, no one had noticed her standing there doing something she knew she shouldn't be doing. She looked in the window again.

"What the hell did you do that for?" Jewel protested.

Donnie looked at the floor. "It's wrong. Wrong."

"What's wrong is breaking something that's not yours."

"I'm sorry. I am sorry." He rubbed his forehead with his hand. His chest felt better, the tightness had eased and he took a deep breath. Yes, he was still breathing. He smiled wryly. "It sure felt good, though."

Jewel's scowl faded. "Be glad I'm moving or I'd have you picking up the pieces with your teeth."

"I believe it." Donnie looked down at her. She was still beautiful. He still wanted her. "I'm sorry."

"I know."

"For it all."

Dante watched the two leave the small bedroom, then walked to the front of the trailer. I should go, she thought, standing near the front door. Walk down that gravel road and pretend I don't know a thing about this. No one would ever know I'd been here. Hearing the door open, she stepped back into the shadows. As long as no one turns a light on, I'll be all right, she thought, wiping a dirty hand on her jeans. Donnie was less than ten feet away, and Dante could see him take his jacket from Jewel.

"Is it going to work out?"

"With Dante?" She sighed. "No, I don't think so."

He stood on the top step and pulled on his jacket. "You love her, don't you?"

"Yes."

"She loves you, too?"

"She says she does. But it's not enough."

"I love you."

"No, you don't, Donnie. To me, I'm me; to you I'm a hallucination."

"That's enough for me," he whispered, his eyes gleaming with tears.

For a moment Jewel thought that the cliché was suddenly true: Eyes really could shine like stars.

Dante watched Donnie walk from Jewel's trailer. He moved slowly, his head down. She had the impulse to follow him, catch him as he turned the corner at the bottom of the drive; she wanted to walk next to him, not saying anything, not a single word, but to walk step by step with him. Instead, she went back to the window to stand at the edge of the light, the hedge catching on her clothes.

Jewel stood in her bedroom, staring at the mess. Seven years' bad luck for Donnie James. I wonder what the penalty is for being in the same room when it happens? Please, no more bad luck. I'm not as tough as I once thought I was.

Dante studied her lover. A wistfulness drifted over her like a mist. What would she give to look over to see Jewel asleep in her narrow bed for the last time, the wrinkled sheet pushed away to expose a breast, her hair tangled and lips still full from kissing and biting in the dark? Should I be with her, Dante thought, waking up with her instead of waking up to feel lost and lost and lost? Should I be holding her, not standing outside of her life looking in?

There's only a window between us, which I could break easily. It's only glass.

Impulsively, she turned from the window, intent on Jewel. The tangled branches and the damp grass fought against her. Dante slipped, regained her balance, slipped again and fell.

Alma could get a new mirror. Most of the glass was even caught under the empty vanity, shining like pools of water and not even a threat to bare feet. The bedroom was still her bedroom, the bed still her bed, but Jewel knew she wouldn't sleep there again. She wasn't even sure if she would sleep anywhere the rest of the night, since her peace was as shattered as the mirror. There was another bed, but her mother had died in it, and not even Jewel had the courage to lie there.

The rain of several days seeped into Dante's clothes as she lay on the ground. The pain below her eye was blunt like a bruise and tingling sharply like nettles at the same time. For a moment, she pressed the wound with her palm, rocketing color through her vision.

"Help me," she gasped, too softly for anyone to hear. Help. It hurts, it hurts. How bad is it? Have I lost this eye, too? Breath ragged and teeth clenched, she pulled her hand from her face.

Jewel reached under the vanity carefully to get the broken glass. The very least she could do was throw out the larger pieces. The edges were wicked, seeming to hold the promise of violence and pain.

Dante blinked. Even that small action caused the tear across her cheekbone to burn. She could see. The branches had missed her eye. Blood was warm on her skin. She blinked again. Already it was starting to swell. Some ice, she thought, aware that her whole body seemed to be burning and that there was a film of sweat on her face and neck. Her arm muscles trembled and her breath was harsh in her ears. Her palm and fingers were spattered with blood. She was sure the side of her face was, too. Untucking her T-shirt, she pressed the end to the wound.

Taking the shards of glass and the broken candles, Jewel set them carefully in an empty box outside the bedroom door. I have to remember to throw that away when I leave, she thought, staring at her own broken reflection in all the pieces.

Then Dante noticed the jagged limb that she had fallen against. In the gold light, she saw a drop of blood roll slowly off the tip and down the side toward the ground, as if it were bleeding. She braced herself for a wail or whisper of pain, but there was only the murmur of the rain.

fifteen

•

DONNIE REALIZED THE night was quiet. So was the Empire when he stepped inside. If I turn on the lights, he considered, somebody will notice and come over here. He chose the dark.

Creeping up the stairs, he kept one hand on the railing till he got to the top. The door to the projection booth was unlocked, and he stepped in. Beneath his feet, he crushed loops and loops of *Gaslight*, the sound reminding him of stepping on a dried-out beetle in the summer. Who the hell turned off the projector like this? The film's all over the goddamn place, he thought, leaning over to pick it up, then standing straight again. He knew he should pick up the movie circling all over the floor, knew he should clean it, repair it and rewind it, but there was no use. Donnie James Champlin wasn't going to be handling movies for the Empire or anybody else.

Digging into his pocket, he pulled out a wooden match and struck it on the wall. It flared into life, for a moment making *Gaslight* twitch and slither like a huge, narrow snake on the floor. Donnie shifted carefully and balanced on his toes. While he knew he would never touch film again, it was senseless to cause more damage to it. By matchlight, the booth seemed bigger and the ceiling higher. The steel of the projectors glittered in the dim light. The windows that looked into the theater were blacker than ever, as if there were no glass in them at all to catch the small flame's reflection.

Donnie clenched his teeth. When you got to move, you got to move, he thought, standing still in the room. What other choice do you have? The paintings are destroyed, I can smell the smoke in my clothes. I don't even need to close my eyes to see fire dancing across the pictures, the tongues of the flames like streamers as the fire seemed to go crazy with joy. It licks and pauses, thrusting out here and there, then wrapping the paintings in destructive red-and-gold ribbon. Now they're nothing but a black pile of ash, and I swear to god, from now on I'll always carry matches as a reminder.

The match was burning low. He dug another out of his pocket and lit it by the flame of the first. It burst into white-gold, then calmed to a cheerful yellow. The first match he blew out and set carefully on the counter next to his set of keys.

Jewel was going. He knew there was no way he would remain in town without her. For a moment, he had the urge to run back to her house and force a promise that she'd stay. His chest started to tighten again. For a moment he could see them, living a passionate life of love and hate that would tear them apart and bring them back together. Jewel would be his personal fury, his inspiration, his creation and his nemesis. She would make him a worse man but a better artist; it was an acceptable trade. Like D. H. Lawrence and Frieda, Van Gogh and the girl that got his ear, Abelard and Heloise, they would share a great love.

Donnie shook his head. He had thought of her so long, so often, that she had worn a deep groove into his mind. I did love her. I still do. I think maybe I always will. But she doesn't love me, she will never love me. All my life I thought the worst thing that could happen to a man was to become another Wrong-Way Corrigan, but now I know. All my life I thought the second worst would be to be forgotten. Now I see that the very worst is to love where there is no room for it; to love where there is no room for me.

I could hate her. I could. Dropping his head, he inhaled, breathing the smell of fire. But what's the use? I'll end with my heart smoldering and each breath a sulky smoke that forces my eyes to close and my throat to burn. So I'll go away. I'll go to the sea. The sea seems to be a well-excavated grave—where else could I go to lose the thought of her? Where else can I toss in this memory and desire, and know they will drop away?

Donnie blew out the match in his fingers. He left the second match next to the first and walked out of the small room, closing the door carefully behind him. He was finished with the Empire and the Empire was finished with him. His hand slipped lightly down the banister, his feet bounded across the diamond carpet of the lobby for the last time. Stuffing his hands into his pockets, he felt the wooden matches he still had left. Fire is a useful thing, Donnie James Champlin thought, looking through the glass door between him and the night. Amazing how the force of fire, a weightless element, can claim the beginnings and endings of a thing.

sixteen

•

Jewel turned the corner and walked quickly toward the Empire.
Dante was leaving her. Someday, Jewel hoped, she would think of
her without that ache. Their first kiss ever was witnessed by stars
and snow in the mountains outside Tahoe. Their first kiss here, in
this small town, was witnessed by the rain. The drops, crystal petals
of a strange flower, passed the lovers and fell on the wet ground.
The earth was full of water, too full for these drops. So the small
witnesses lay on the grass and the cement steps of the mobile home,
while the lovers walked indoors to remember the touch of each
other.

Would anybody remember her and Dante? It seemed no one had
even noticed them, except Donnie of course. It seemed no one in
town stayed here long enough to capture and embroider the stories.
She thought, outrageous stories, like my dancing in Tahoe, certainly made the rounds, but it seems that no one bothered to bend
facts into some sort of legendary truth. Perhaps they have all lost
their imaginations. Then again, it's a lot of work to tell stories, true
or false, and rain can beat out every ambition. Maybe that's it.
Maybe the rain is keeping the secrets, draining them out of people's

houses and skin and dropping them bit by bit into the ground. Maybe the earth isn't too full of rain, but getting too full of stories.

Jewel looked up and down the street. There was a light on in the Diamond Cafe, a shallow fluorescent at the back. Marlene scrubbing away at nonexistent dirt and hoping for sleep.

This was Jewel's last errand. The house keys were at home on the kitchen table along with some money for the broken mirror and a note for Alma. Shifting her suitcase to her left hand, she pulled out her key to the Empire and was about to drop it in the mail slot when she noticed that one of the tall lobby doors was unlocked. Who could be here? Jewel wondered as she pulled it open. Could be Virgil. Maybe he just forgot to lock up. She looked around the quiet theater. I should just set my key on the concession counter and leave. I should walk out of here, lock the door and drop the key in the mail slot like I planned. And that would be it. Finished.

The streetlights reflected bluish white in the chrome-angel light fixtures. She sniffed. The air smells funny, different. Maybe Dante was right, she thought. Maybe the place is on fire. She sniffed again, glancing around. There's definitely something, but as long as it doesn't go up in flames while I'm here, I don't give a damn, she decided, crossing the lobby.

She pushed open the wooden door into the main floor and took an aisle seat in the last row. The darkness pressed against her eyes. She could see the vague outline of the screen ahead of her. This place is full of outlines and shadows, all hazy reminders of what's beneath the surface, just like Icarus tumbling from the ceiling and the water stains not letting a woman forget that rain will always fall.

I have decided, she thought, rubbing the back of her neck, that I hate movies. Movies full of lies, movies that are lies, movies that people believe in because they're more like real life than real life. Just like *D.O.A.* and *Gaslight*. Either you're fighting against time and the inevitable conclusion of death for a stupid reason, or someone is trying to drive you nuts. Can I trust life or the universe?

Of course not. Is it true that what goes around comes around? No. There are only imperfect circles and imperfect strangers. Like Dante thinks, only gravity keeps us sticking to the earth, and gravity isn't acting out of kindness or a sense of duty like the angels with their light fixtures. Gravity pulls at me because I happen to be in the way.

And love. It tears you wide open and the sorrow of everyday living accumulates in the exposed places. It is the price. The endless combinations of sadness like a late-spring frost wrapping around the blossoms of a tree. Beautiful and destructive. Dante is right. To love only leaves you sadder. Leaves you open and broken. With my mama, what I thought was a pearl made of love was only the clutter of everyday living. It was gravity. Gravity that's not restricted to planets and suns, but the gravity we all have.

Jewel got to her feet. A weariness dragged at her as she picked up her suitcase and walked up the aisle. There was a bus heading south that she could catch on the highway. It would be a cold hour of waiting, but it was better than staying here. So much easier to leave than to be left, she knew. So much easier to be the beloved than the lover. Like me and Donnie. Like Dante and me.

She pushed open the door to the lobby and caught it as it closed so there would be no sound of her leaving. What is the use of even examining Dante and me? Love isn't enough. There is no home for anyone, only small stops under siege. Illusion. Lies. Love won't protect you from ghosts, love won't stop the illusion that you can grip the solid ground and last forever. Nothing lasts forever. Nothing lasts, period. Like the rain, love is constantly moving, changing shape and falling elsewhere.

Oh, god. Jewel's breath came out in a gasp. I am tired. I am tired of loving, I am tired of lust, I am tired of performing magic by crushing life and hope and memory together till they become interchangeable. I am tired to my bones. Since Mama's death, I have borrowed strength from the future. Picking a casket, choosing flowers, fending off the preacher offered by the funeral home, following some customs and defying others gave me strength. But now I think I'm finally empty.

Why? she asked silently, opening the tall glass door. Why have I become so weak? I used up what I had, thinking I could find something to replace it. I can see that now, just as I can see that ghosts and gods are invented to convince people that the universe is crowded with living things waiting to do a good turn. But they don't exist. We are alone, all incredibly alone.

Jewel stepped into the night, locking the door to the Empire behind her and leaving the memories and angels. The street was dark now; the light in the cafe was out. I hope Marlene can get to sleep, she thought, taking a deep breath. I hope she at least has gotten what she wants. Stepping to the ticket window, Jewel dropped her key to the theater into the mail slot.

An hour to kill until the bus arrived. Jewel stood perfectly still on the sidewalk, glancing up at the few stars visible. They were points of hope no longer—no longer a shelter or a tapestry full of pictures and stories. They were only stars now. There was no more up and down, here and there, right and wrong. There was only away. Her stomach churned. Only the tightest grip she could get on the suitcase kept her in place.

So now Dante will know what it means to be left behind. I don't wish that pain on her, but I can't heap more of it on top of what I got. Not now. Not here. Maybe next week, next month, next year; maybe in the next town or the next county or my next home. I will get strong again in another time and place. I will. I will fix my heart.

With a deep breath, Jewel turned her eyes from the sky, hunched deeper into her jacket and walked slowly down the street.

seventeen

•

COMING BACK FROM Jewel's, her T-shirt pressed to the side of her face, Dante had noticed the fluorescent light at the Diamond Cafe. They have ice, was her first thought. Who the hell would be in there at this time of night? was her second. Peering in through the front window, she could see Marlene as she bent over the stainless-steel counter. Coffee and iced-tea machines, stacks of glasses, salt and pepper shakers, everything that had been on the counter that afternoon was shoved aside so Marlene, both arms covered to the elbows in suds, could scrub. Dante pounded on the door.

"More dramatic than deep," Marlene announced after cleaning the cut. "The iodine will help against infection but you should go to the doctor to get something."

"I don't want to."

"Don't be foolish. Don't drive up there yourself; have somebody drive you into Susanville."

"It isn't necessary." The iodine had screamed into the wound, causing Dante to break into another sweat and hold on to the Formica lunch counter with both hands. Now she was grateful for the cold shock of the ice bag against her bruised skin.

Marlene pressed her lips together as she held up the gauze and tape bandage she'd made. "Don't push your luck, Dante. Another quarter of an inch . . . well, you don't want an infection and you might want somebody to make sure nothing important is damaged."

"It'll be fine." Dante saw the older woman's determination. "All right. I'll have somebody take a look at it."

Satisfied, Marlene taped the bandage over the wound.

"I don't know how to thank you."

"Too bad you're not a Gypsy or you could tell me my future for free."

"That is too bad, because I would."

"So why don't you tell me what your real name is? You said the other day Dante isn't it, so spill your guts."

Twisting on the stool where she was sitting, Dante looked at her hand. The blood had dried, leaving lines of rust in her skin.

"You're not one of those Du Ponts or Rockefellers trying to run away from all that money, are you?"

Dante laughed. It made her cheek hurt. "No."

"Thank god for that. You the child of somebody famous? Some big movie star?"

She shook her head and smiled. That hurt, too. "My name is Clio."

"Clio? Like Cleopatra?"

Cleopatra, with her fondness for sticking pins into the breasts of slave girls? "No. Clio, as in the advertising awards. My dad made TV commercials. My name is Clio Federico Burke."

"Clio Federico Burke," Marlene repeated, nodding. "What's wrong with that? Clio is very pretty. Very feminine."

"Nobody ever called me Clio. When I was little, my older brother—"

"The one who rode motorcycles?"

"Yeah. He was going through an intellectual phase and was reading *The Divine Comedy*. My dad told him it was time for bed, and Robbie said he was in the middle of a great book and he just had to finish it. My dad asked him what he was reading. Dante, Robbie says. My dad was impressed and Rob got to stay up late. The next night my dad tells me to go upstairs and go to sleep. I said that I was reading this great book and just had to finish it. I think I was reading *Go Dog, Go!* or something. So my dad asks me just what is it that I can't put down, and I answer very seriously, 'Dante.' "

"And that's it?"

"That's it."

"Here I was expecting a kidnapping or a cult brainwashing or at least a witness protection program and what do I get? Poetry. Intellectuals. TV commercials. Nicknames." Marlene picked up the scrub brush from the stainless-steel counter and dipped it into a bucket. "They aren't looking for you, are they?"

"My family? No."

"Anybody else looking for you?" Marlene grinned slyly. "The law? Maybe those guys in the white coats?"

Dante shook her head. "Sorry."

"So I can't even hope that I might see you on one of those TV shows." Pulling the brush out, she sloshed suds all over and began scrubbing. "I was thinking about that the other night. Just what I would do if I saw one of those wanted people. I swear to god I once had a dishwasher who looked like Jimmy Hoffa. I almost called the FBI but Henry told me not to worry. He said that if our dishwasher was Jimmy Hoffa, he was a lot better off in our cafe than out there tangling with the Mafia."

Dante watched as Marlene began drying the counter with a towel. "You want some help?"

Marlene shook her head. "I do this mostly as hypnosis. Brush in the bucket, brush on the counter, back and forth three, five or seven times, back to the bucket, then dry off the counter."

Dante nodded.

"I used to drink till I fell asleep. Did I ever tell you? I got insomnia real bad and that used to be the way I'd take care of it. Most people drink for fun or misery or habit, but I'd drink to get to sleep. At first. Then things started getting out of hand, you know? Suddenly drinking was all that mattered."

Dropping the brush into the bucket, Marlene held up her nail-bitten right hand. "I don't have much sensation anymore. Brain damage, they say. My fingers move fine but they're numb. I miss the touch of some things—sprinkling salt out of my palm, smoothing a sheet, the cold sides of a glass in summer, Henry's face when he needs a shave."

Marlene's hand fell slowly to the counter, pink from the soapy water and the work. For a moment, Dante wanted very much to reach over and hold it.

"You know, he stuck by me through it all. Most men wouldn't. But Henry, he'd do anything for me and I'd do anything for him. We moved here after I sobered up nine years ago. Nine years. About a year ago I started having this trouble sleeping again."

Dante studied Marlene's face. She could see now where years, boozing and sleeplessness had drawn themselves.

"I think it's the worry. Trying to pay the bills, trying to get a little in the bank, the usual sorts of things you start to think about. I start wondering how much it's all going to cost and if we can pay and what happens if we can't. Some nights I lie there staring at the ceiling as if I expect the whole ball of trouble to fall through on top of us." Marlene laughed softly and leaned against the counter with her hand on her hip. "Just listen to me going on and on. Is the ice helping, honey?"

"Yeah. Thanks."

"Sure." Marlene carried the bucket to a shallow sink in the middle of the wall. "Let me tell you something. I've been pretty lucky, sleep or no sleep. Lots of people got only one thread to cling to. If something comes along to snip that thread, down they fall and it's a long drop into craziness. In my case, I got work. That's worth something. And I got Henry. The kind of love we got. You got love, too, don't you?"

"Yeah," Dante answered slowly. "I do."

Marlene smiled and emptied the bucket. "I knew it. Not much gets by these tired old eyes. She's a nice girl, that Jewel. I admire her determination."

"So do I," Dante said softly. She handed Marlene the ice bag. "Thank you. I have to go now."

"I'll go with you. I think I'm done for the night."

Dante stood on the walk as Marlene locked the door to the dark cafe. How fast can I get to Jewel? she wondered.

"You ever heard of that valerian Bernie was talking about?" Marlene asked quietly.

"Yeah."

"Does it work?"

"I've heard it does."

"Huh. Well, maybe I'll have Henry drive up to the Susanville mall to get some."

"Maybe you should do that," Dante agreed, her throat suddenly tight. "Good night, Marlene."

Marlene nodded. "Good-bye, Dante."

The night was quiet. Dante watched Marlene turn the corner and disappear from view. I've got the kind of love she means. Marlene has known it all along, while I've been too stupid to see it. Turning on her heel, she hurried down the street, the sound of her boots echoing in the quiet. She passed her motorcycle parked in the street, the front wheel pointing out, ready to leave.

After the third time she pounded on the door to the mobile home, she stepped inside. Jewel wasn't there. There's only one place she can be, Dante concluded. She rushed back to the Empire, the cut on her cheekbone throbbing.

The door was unlocked. Dante had guessed right; somewhere in the gloom of the Empire, Jewel was sitting in the dark. Dante twitched her cheek. Already the bandage Marlene had taped on was itching. She pulled in a deep breath. The smell of metal, grease and salt twisted and spilled over her like genies trying to escape. The Empire did not smell musty like the yellowing lace on a wedding dress or the wool suit of a dead man turning to dust. Mostly it was decay sifting between the odor of hot popcorn, a scent distinctly belonging to something alive that is dying. She had read that when Humphrey Bogart was dying of cancer and had fallen into a coma, people could smell his flesh already rotting. That was the smell, she decided. That was the odor that surrounded her in the Empire Theater.

The slashes of light from the street lamp blinked off anything that would reflect, then seeped like rain into the carpet. Such oblique lines and crooked shapes were trademarks of *film noir*. There were no better users of chiaroscuro than the Germans after World War II. Deciding to paint life and movies black, the filmmakers filled the human eye with uneasiness. A character you were supposed to trust was cut with ribbons of light, faces were blocked by shadow and scenes were filled with hopelessness in the face of destiny. Dante had thought of *film noir* as the modern version of ancient Greek tragedy with a twist: There were no gods after World War II.

She lit a cigarette, took two steps forward in the darkness, then stopped again. Jewel came to be alone, to sit and think or whatever it was she wants to do. Do I love her? Yes. Do I want her? Yes. Do we stand a chance together in this world? No. Suddenly, Dante could feel that she was now able to look at things rather than watch out for them. The fire that they shared had burned away the fear. What medicine does not cure, the iron does. What the iron doesn't cure, fire exterminates.

I see it now, she thought. It's become a picture with sharp edges intact. Like a forest fire that could save people from themselves, this love can rescue me. It's more than a thread to hold onto. This love is all that is worthwhile. This fire has burned away the fear of searching forever and finding nothing. People who say there is a natural justice are wrong. People who say that the search is most important are wrong. Once you have decided to continue living, you must decide what it is that will keep you here. It is love. It is fire. The heat and light we share is what keeps me on this earth. Love isn't a promise. It's not a lock to be picked. Love is a mistake. Love is undependable. If the steadiest person is unreliable in love, then the unsteady are positively dangerous. Love is the best mistake to make. It's splintered sunshine through lead-paned windows. It's a single note vibrating through leaves blown by the wind.

Gravity and love are the only things keeping me on the earth— the first is indifferent, the second is near impossible. But I have my chance. So many people trade a chance at desire for nothing. Nothing. What can compare with fire?

Fire. Love. What am I missing, then? The ability to endure. To simply wait it out. To believe, not only in my own survival, but in the survival of someone else, and in what we share, what is both me and not me. This love. This fire. The faith to believe I can endure every splash of humiliation and defeat, every gust of sour disappointment, and be able to bring the flame back to life. Two pairs of hands shield the spark of it. To endure to burn for each other again. How could such a thing be true and how could a woman walk wide-eyed into it?

I do love Jewel. I have been so far away from such light and such warmth. But to endure. It is a talent you don't know you have until you have reason for it. It's like a tightrope stretched from the roof of a burning building, and you're not sure you have the balance until the time comes to cross. Some people are born with it. Some people develop it. And some people never feel the lack. But I've never had to endure for someone other than me. Someone alive. Robbie died at the age of seventeen, when Todd Nielsen's VW Bug smashed into a telephone pole. My father checked into a small motel off the highway to commit suicide. I never blamed my brother for dying and I never blamed my father for shooting himself. But they never taught me how to love against the odds. I never learned how to say yes and make it stick.

So now I'll learn. Jewel will teach me.

My stuff is packed. I'm ready to leave and to take her with me. I'll ride back to her trailer and wait for her, Dante decided, flicking her cigarette away. It hopped over the fire extinguisher Jewel had heaved at the wall, and it landed in a far corner, the ember leaving a red trace that seemed to burn into Dante's sight.

eighteen

•

VIRGIL PICKED UP the fire extinguisher and held it in his big hands. Four feet up from the floor, there was a rectangle of crushed wall. Destruction. Revelation. Even the pagans believe the world is coming to an End. Even the Moslems know Fire and Damnation will ring this earth and burn out the Sin of Mankind. It is no wonder that people are returning to the Holy Book, returning to Christ and the Prophets. We all know, it is coded into our very selves, we human beings have always known such an End was coming. So many refuse to hear the very Truth whispering in their souls. Refuse to obey the Words of God echoing. I have heard Him. I have heard Him as clearly as a bird in the morning, its song resting on the silence as easily as a kind hand on the face of a child. And I can smell Sin in the lobby of this theater. Smell it slithering between the rancid butter and moldy carpet, tying itself into what people believe is harmless. They breathe it in, deep into their lungs to infect the blood. I have seen it. Adulterers groping one another in the darkness, children forgetting all thoughts of Purity to succumb to Evil. I have witnessed it. I condemn it.

Sweat stung the scratches in his face. He hugged the fire extinguisher to his chest. She beguiled me. She is Lilith, a witch sent to devour my 3-In-One Soul. She appeared regular, an ordinary sinner, a typical woman until I saw her; then, as if in a dream, she became more beautiful. I thought it was Holiness blooming, God's Power becoming Manifest, but she is from the Evil One. She feeds on Strength and Righteousness.

I have the gift of Prophecy and I see that Destruction is imminent. I keep the gift silent; such things are not to be held over the heads of others, it is not something to be proud of. I hear God. I speak to Him. I read the Signs. The world is like this wall. The anger of God is like this fire extinguisher going through it. Like a bolt of hurled lightning striking out, out, out. Working through an Instrument of God. I am that Instrument.

Virgil carried the fire extinguisher like a child through the Empire. Below the stage, with sixty years of clutter surrounding him, he would make his sacrifice. The only Sacrifice worth making, he decided.

epilogue

•

WHAT YOU HAVE to know about fire is a lot. The way it changes objects into light. What you need to see is the blue-and-topaz flames reducing something once solid into a vague outline, and then to ash that people breathe into themselves. Learning about burning like St. Theresa and the burning spear, like Johnny Cash and that ring of fire, like Mithra and his worshippers, like Pentecost raining onto apostles. Learning about candles lit in memory, will-o'-the-wisps hanging over new graves, forest fires and burnt offerings.

The Empire caught fire. Almost the whole town gathered around the orange-gold flames throwing sparks at the sky as if trying to replace the stars. Sheriff Bernie Tollett had to keep telling everyone to stay back, but they continued to edge closer to the warmth. Fire, like love, has an all-embracing quality.

The Empire had been showing a double feature that week, *D.O.A.* and *Gaslight*. *D.O.A.* was directed by Rudolph Maté and he'd crammed cruelty, jazz and gin into his movie, only to have the film score run over it like a train through a house. And *Gaslight* with lovely Ingrid Bergman being terrorized into insanity and a

148

villain with a French accent. Both films have a vicious black-and-white studio elegance and are filled with strange angles and paranoia. The uneasiness in either film could cause sparks. Maybe the movies had caused the cyclone burning in the middle of town, though no one could be sure. The fire itself put all thought of guessing and second-guessing out of people's minds. There'd be time enough for that later; tonight, the Empire was putting on its last show.

Marlene and Henry arrived first. She had seen a gold halo hanging over the middle of town. By the time Henry was awake and the volunteer firefighters were at work, flames were lashing the lobby, contained only by the tall glass doors that soon shattered with the heat. Alma Queyar held her baby as her husband Antone helped drag water hoses. They had been packing all weekend so they could move into the mobile home they'd bought from Jewel Mraz. No one knew where Jewel was, or Donnie James Champlin or Virgil Penhaligan. They worked at the Empire Theater, along with that one-eyed woman who'd been in town for a week. Her motorcycle was gone, meaning she had moved on, but there was a ripple of talk as to why the other three weren't around. The fire lit up the town; who within sight could miss it? Were they caught in the inferno?

The firefighters had no chance against the flames. Even with all the rain that had fallen that week, the wood blazed out with a fury as if it had been waiting for the opportunity. The lights danced off the buildings, making the windows glint like gold teeth. You could tell how hot the fire was when you turned away to let the cold autumn air spill over your face and neck, sending a chill all the way down your back to set you to shivering. The street was dark blue, the air filled with ash and smoke. The roof caved in and sparks fanned out like a handful of careless confetti to be stamped out. It was a complicated dance between burning building, flames, and people crushing the beads of fire scattered on the ground.

Can a place, a silent dark building have the desire to finally end? Can brick and wood and brass feel pain? Do they soak up the emotions around them, the loud fierce emotions of anger, hate, love and revulsion, vibrate with the pictures from the screen and the half-lies people tell one another in the half-darkness? Did the Empire, with its marquee and the neon lights stretching up the tower with "GOD" painted in scarlet at the top, give in to the destruction latent in everyone and everything?

The fire showed the street as half a circle, almost a world unto itself. Occasionally, a strong blast of flame would leap higher, sending a dart of light that caused anything of light shade to respond in kind. Faces. Shirt fronts. The people standing around it were decked with gold, their features suddenly more alive as the blaze danced over them, and things with no particular polish were glazed. Eyes glowed like lanterns. The windows reflecting the fire seemed alive, while those farther down the street stayed cold and still in the darkness.